I0659523

HARD

Work

K.M. SCOTT

Books by K.M. Scott writing as Gabrielle Bisset

Blood Avenged (Sons of Navarus #1)
Blood Betrayed (Sons of Navarus #2)
Longing (A Sons of Navarus Short Story)
Blood Spirit (Sons of Navarus #3)
The Deepest Cut (A Sons of Navarus Short Story)
Blood Prophecy (Sons of Navarus #4)
Blood Craving (Sons of Navarus #5)
Blood Eclipse (Sons of Navarus #6)

Stolen Destiny (Destined Ones Duology #1)
Destiny Redeemed (Destined Ones Duology #2)

Love's Master
Masquerade
The Victorian Erotic Romance Trilogy

Hard Work is a work of fiction. Names, characters, places, and events are the products of the author's imagination. Any resemblance to events, locations, or persons, living or dead, is coincidental.

2017 Copper Key Media, LLC
Print Edition

Copyright © 2017 Copper Key Media, LLC

All rights reserved. Without limiting the rights under copyright reserved above, no part of this publication may be reproduced, stored in or introduced into a retrieval system, or transmitted, in any form, or by any means (electronic, mechanical, photocopying, recording, or otherwise) without the prior written permission of the copyright owner.

Published in the United States

ISBN: 978-1-941594-78-0

Book Cover design by Sweet 'N Spicy Designs

HARD WORK

Zane Gilford has lived a blessed life. The only son of the owner of The Gilford House Inn, he's benefitted from his mother's extraordinary success. But Vermont was never where he wanted to be, and the day after graduation, he put the quaint country inn and everything about it behind him and never looked back.

Until now.

The death of his mother left Zane a very wealthy man, but in her will she also left him a surprise. For an entire year, he must run that Vermont inn he's hated all his life if he wants to get one red cent of his inheritance.

Becca Fox has worked her way to the top of the advertising business and has the personal and professional scars to prove it. In her rare time off, she loves visiting her favorite bed and breakfast in the mountains of Vermont. When she finds a new owner running The Gilford House Inn, she wonders if her favorite getaway place has been ruined for her. He's sexy as all hell and incredibly good looking, but he's so cocky and arrogant.

From the first moment he sees her, Zane knows he wants Becca, but to get a woman like her, he's going to have to learn to be a better man than he's ever been. He's got an inn to run and a woman to win. Neither is going to be easy. And time isn't in his favor.

CHAPTER ONE

Zane

EVERY GUY KNOWS when he meets The One. Even guys like me, who don't believe anything like that exists, have to admit when the girl of their dreams walks into their life.

The moment I saw Becca Fox I knew she was that for me. She was beautiful, smart, and sexy.

And she wanted me.

Like every day that summer, I waited for her to get out of work at the diner where she waitressed to take her home so she could get a shower before we headed out for another night together. What had started as complete lust between two people at a party in late May had grown into a relationship I didn't want to ever end.

I knew she'd go back to college in a couple weeks, but until then, I planned on spending every moment I could with her. In just a few months, she'd became as important to me as the air I breathed.

And even more, she loved me.

Go figure. A beautiful and intelligent woman wanting me, Zane Gilford.

She bounded out the front door of Dante's Diner and walked toward me so full of life and as excited to see me as I was to see her. "Hey, you! When are you going to finally come inside one day and wait for me at the counter? I make a mean root beer float, you know."

The cute way she smiled when she said that made me want to take her in my arms and never let her go. Leaning down to kiss her hello, I said, "Maybe tomorrow. It's a nice day out, so I thought I'd hang out here and wait for you."

Becca tilted her head back and closed her eyes to feel the hot August sun on her face for the first time that day. "This whole working from six in the morning to noon is for the birds."

I pulled her close to me and inhaled the sickeningly greasy smell of her uniform. But even that couldn't make me want to let her go. "At least it lets us spend a lot of time together. What do you want to do today?"

She lowered her head and beamed one of her beautiful smiles up at me. "After I get a shower so I don't stink like fried food, I'd love to just go to your apartment and lay in your arms while we sit on your balcony."

"Are you sure? We can go anywhere you want," I said, tucking her dark hair back behind her left ear.

"I'm sure. I just want to spend the day in your arms listening to the ocean below."

That sounded like heaven to me, even though I would have taken her anywhere she wanted. All she had to do was ask.

I kissed her softly and smiled. "Whatever you want. As long as we're together, that's all that matters."

As we walked toward my car parked a block away, she told me about the customers she'd encountered that day and I listened, hanging on every word. I'd never thought this kind of everyday stuff could make me so happy, but I knew the real reason I'd never been happier in my life was because I had Becca with me.

So while she chatted about customers and their bizarre requests that made her way too little money in tips, I swore to myself that I'd never let her go. If I did, I'd be the most miserable man alive.

CHAPTER TWO

Zane

I SAT ALONE in the cramped law office of Mitchell Worthington, a name that sounded far more impressive than the man who bore it was. The place reminded me of everything I hated about that Podunk town in Vermont. It was musty, old, and much like the ancient and yellowed computer on the lawyer's desk, useless. Other than maple syrup and leaves, it didn't offer anything to the average American, and I was well beyond average.

My mother's lawyer walked in and gingerly sat down in his office chair. An old man with white hair and eyebrows a horned owl might balk at, it took him a full minute to get settled and finally look across the desk at me.

"Mr. Gilford, I'd like to start by extending my sympathies. Your mother was a good woman, and I'm sorry she's passed. It seems like just yesterday that she came here looking for an attorney to represent her business interests. She was a glowing woman who brought joy to those around her. She will be sorely missed."

I nodded because I had to. He and I both knew I wasn't there for some therapy session.

Not getting the reaction he wanted, he continued. "Right, okay, let me see. Yes, let me look at some of the paperwork here." Thumbing through the stack of papers, he said, "Yes…okay, that's what I need."

Instead of actually telling me what I wanted to hear, he sat silently reading over the document for nearly a minute before looking up at me. "Well, Mr. Gilford, you'll be pleased to know she's left you everything. However, there is one caveat, and I feel I must prepare you by saying that you are not going to like it."

I sighed and rolled my eyes. There was always something else when it came to my mother. Even in death, she had a way of making things annoying, like requiring me to meet her lawyer in person for this crap when I should have been back enjoying my life in California, not in Vermont where I could already smell the stench of old people and hipsters all over me.

"Fine. What's the caveat?" I asked after her lawyer sat quietly waiting for me to respond.

"Mr. Gilford, your mother has stipulated that if you are to receive a penny of her substantial fortune, you'll be required to run The Gilford House Inn successfully for one year. That means at the end of that year, it cannot be in a worse state financially than it was when you inherited it, which is today. After a year, you will receive her fortune in full and may do what you please. She's left a letter explaining it all here for you."

The old man pushed the envelope toward me. Even that mannerism was painfully slow, and I wanted to just snatch it out of his hands. Then the full effect of what the officious bastard had just said hit me. I sat there in shock, unable to speak as my new reality sunk into my brain.

"The Gilford House Inn has indeed taken off in these past years, Mr. Gilford. Your mother ran a darned good business, and coupled with her ability to invest wisely, led a productive life. You'll be well taken care of for it. In fact, my wife and I stayed at The Gilford House Inn a few years ago, and I can tell you it was the best vacation we've had in ages. We try to go back every year now, in fact, and it gets better and better each time. I think you'll especially enjoy the…"

I slammed the palm of my hand hard on the desk, startling the man as his ridiculous collection of folksy knickknacks and pictures of his grandchildren rattled between us.

"Is this for real? I don't give a damn about her little hole-in-the-wall motel! Can she actually put this in her will? Will this bullshit hold up in court? This has got to be some kind of sick joke. I can't just take over some fleabag motel that I know nothing about. There has to be a way out of this!" I said, practically growling with anger.

I couldn't believe this shit. My mother had known since I was a kid just how much I had hated that damned place. Sure, I had played there and enjoyed games of hide and seek in the hallways and the stairways as a child, but I'd loathed and despised that money pit since I was old enough to know better.

Though apparently, it hadn't been as bad an investment as I'd thought. I didn't begrudge her any success she may have had with the place. Good for her that she'd found success with it. Still, the notion of me running the place was nothing less than ridiculous.

Old man Worthington nodded, his eyebrows moving with his head as he said, "Yes, I put together the will with her, and it all checks out legally, so you better settle in, Mr. Gilford. You've got a year to do what she wanted. Otherwise, you aren't getting a dime. Now I know this might seem overwhelming, but she left very detailed instructions so you can slide into the role of owner very easily. We worked together for weeks to ensure your easy transition."

I shook my head and balled my fists at my

sides. "She can't do that. I'm her only child. That money has to go somewhere."

I was grasping at straws, but I hoped if I confronted him that would make him cave and give me the money. "It's not like you have any loyalty to her wishes, so what do you care? You're just some lawyer."

Worthington nodded again and answered after pausing for an insufferable amount of time. "Well, she did set aside a quarter of a million to be given to various charities. If you cannot fulfill the requirements outlined in her will, the money will automatically go to them. As for my caring, not only is this my job, Mr. Gilford, but ensuring your mother's final wishes come to pass is also a privilege. She was a wonderful woman who worked hard for those she knew and deserved that in return."

My mother and her charities. Over my dead body would strangers get what was rightfully mine.

He pointed at the envelope on the desk in front of me. "It's all in there. She made sure to be quite explicit with her wishes. If you have any more questions, I can help you or I can put you in contact with…"

I didn't feel like hearing anything else from the old man. I knew he wasn't going to help me anyway, so I walked out on him, slamming the door behind me and startling the tacky twenty-something with a bad dye job behind the receptionist's desk.

As I stepped outside and off the curb, I nearly got run over by some teal antique car and scowled angrily at the idiot driving it. An old man with a hat, like eighty percent of the population in Burlington, Vermont. They must have been importing them from the West coast because I'd already seen more old men in hats in Vermont than I had in all the years I'd spent in California.

I threw him a nasty look and slid into the driver's seat of my Mercedes to read my mother's letter to me.

My Dearest Zane,

If you are reading this, we never got the chance to talk before my death. For that, I am truly sorry. I leave this world with a host of regrets, but none more than what I did to you. My only child, you were blessed with everything good, and I believed it was my duty as your mother to give you everything I could. I know now that was a mistake.

I hope in death I will be able to give you what I did not in life. To that end, I am leaving you the inn. You will have to learn to work with the staff to ensure its success. You've never been very adept at tolerating others, but you will have to accept that people aren't all like you if you ever want to inherit my money. Be good to them, Zane, and they will be good to you in return. I know you never believed me, but they are family. I hope you come to see that as I did.

Zane, I loved you, but I made mistakes giving you everything as you were growing up. I'm doing this in the hopes that I can compensate for all I didn't do to teach you right. I hope you succeed. I believe with all my heart you will.

Love,
Mom

She had to be kidding.

I crumpled up the letter into a tight ball and whipped it at the passenger side window before tossing the packet Worthington had given me onto the floor behind me. It contained the relevant documents and information for running that rat hole of an inn, but it wasn't anything I cared about at that moment.

Leave it to my mother to make her death worse than it already was.

I closed my eyes and thought of the time when I was sixteen and came home from boarding school on Christmas break to that crappy inn. It was already buried under too much snow, and I spent much of my so-called vacation in my room playing video games and pretending I was somewhere else. I'd avoided my mother for the most part, and it had been working out just fine until I heard her call my name from outside in the hall.

"Zane, sweetheart, will you come out, please? I'd love to see you downstairs in the dining room."

I'd already figured out by that age that running the place kept her busy enough that if I ignored her the first or second time she called, she'd go away. Inevitably, some issue would crop up or some guest would want to thank her for something she'd done and she would leave me alone and more than likely forget whatever it was she had initially wanted me for.

Still, for whatever reason, I was curious, so I walked out of my room and into the hall to find out what she wanted.

"Honey, please come downstairs," she called from the dining room as I stood stubbornly in the hallway above. "We have a few new additions to our team this Christmas, and I thought we could all decorate the big Christmas tree together! You're going to love Bill here. He's a Warriors fan just like you!"

I listened to a man mutter something, and I rolled my eyes and stayed silent.

"Zane Gilford, I know you can hear me. Come down here and meet Bill. It would be nice for you to talk to someone while you're here. Maybe you'll have a nice story to take back and tell the boys at school."

I'd always hated it when she used that sickly sweet tone with me. She could have a real attitude when she wanted to, but she wanted to save face for the strangers she called our family. Uninterested in her attempt at creating some quaint holiday tradition, I remained where I stood and waited for the situation to pass so I could go back to doing what I wanted.

"Zane, get down here now, please."

I'd stormed down the stairs and looked her dead in the eye as I snapped, "I don't care about Bill or anyone else in this crappy excuse for a motel, Mom. I could be spending my vacation at school or with Justin and his family in Aspen, but instead, you drag me back to this place every year. I hate it!"

She'd shaken her head and smiled like always. "Honey, your family is here in Vermont. Not just me but everyone who works here. We're all a team. Besides, it's Christmas. Come on. We can all exchange presents after we finish the tree. I think our new chef even made some cookies for everyone. Isn't that nice of him?"

I saw the employees behind her, nervous

about any confrontation as they edged their way to the back of the room. It was smart of them. That's where they belonged. At sixteen, I had more education than half of them and had already decided what kind of people I was going to surround myself with, and they weren't it.

"Yeah, you want to give me the best gift of all? Send me back so I don't have to hang out with you and these losers on Christmas!"

I stormed back upstairs and spent the rest of the vacation waiting to go back to boarding school where people who I liked existed.

She'd never understood that those people weren't our family. Hell, they weren't even friends. You didn't pay friends and family to come by every day and clean up the sheets. Those people weren't like us, and she could never get that through her skull. They were employees, the literal help, not our family.

My dad had died when I was ten, and ever since then, she'd tried to fill whatever hole in her heart that he'd left with that goddamned inn. I was constantly being introduced to new employees, and when they inevitably left, it was always devastating to my mother. As if anyone wanted to work in the service industry forever, other than her.

I punched my steering wheel as I let go of that memory and focused on the present. Her idea was ridiculous. What was I supposed to gain from a year in that shit hole other than an even deeper loathing of it and Vermont as a whole? It was just like my mother to leave the world with one more annoying task on her list for me.

Putting the car into drive, I peeled away from the curb with another angry punch to the steering wheel that left my hand throbbing. I drove to the last place I wanted to be for even a minute, let alone an entire year, so that I could claim my rightful inheritance.

It was just a year. How bad could that be, right?

A year in a bed and breakfast in Vermont.

God help me.

CHAPTER THREE

Becca

I SLOWLY DROVE up the road that wound its way up the mountain towards The Gilford House Inn, admiring the foliage around me. Red and orange leaves floated down onto my car in a scene of vibrant autumn color. All the best hues of the fall season were out in force on the mountainside as I breathed in the fresh air deeply into my lungs and headed towards my getaway.

I'd picked a great time of the year to get away. Few things in this world were more wonderful than autumn in New England. The gorgeous colors nature put on display combined with the crisp scents the mountains offered couldn't be beat.

Living in Manhattan amid the rat race of New York City had always felt right from the moment I set foot in the city after college, but I hadn't taken the time to step back away from work in far too long. I needed a break, and there was no better place than my favorite country inn.

It was way too easy to let myself get caught up in work for months, even years, on end without giving myself a proper break, but my assistant who doubled as my best friend had finally convinced me that I needed to get out of town for a while and clear my mind.

As she'd put it, "If you walk in that door one more morning, I'm going to carry you out myself. All our projects are caught up, and it's the best time to get away, so please, please go get some rest for yourself!"

She always worried about me, and after some thought, I decided she was right. I needed a break and my favorite little inn tucked away in the mountains of Vermont was the perfect place to get it.

The road gave way to a small gravel parking lot filled with more leaves than gravel at that point in the year. I got out and grabbed my bags, smiling up at the building in front of me. The Gilford House Inn was an enormous white farmhouse style home with a huge wrap-around porch that looked like it had been there since the first Vermont settlers had put down roots and called the area home. It sat atop the mountain like a proud woman, welcoming people to the countryside around it. No matter how much wind, rain, and snow came her way, she never seemed to change at all.

As I walked up the old wooden steps to the front entrance, I grinned as I thought of the creaking that would sound as I took the top stair. My foot landed, and I heard that old, familiar squeak like a welcome back. With a contented sigh, I opened the front door and walked inside.

I'd only met the owner of the inn once and had been tremendously saddened to hear that she'd passed away when my travel agent had mentioned it to me while I was booking my trip. Still, that one meeting sat in my mind as a wonderful memory, and I was immediately aware that she had given the inn much of its lovely personality and warmth. She'd been a bubbly and kind woman who so very clearly adored that inn as more than a building or just a business.

She'd spoken of her inn as though it was her child and had been glowing and excited to brag about all the best people she employed there. I remembered her referring to them as family, and it had warmed my heart to know they had such a fantastic employer.

I walked across the soft carpet toward the large check-in desk and idly wondered to myself if new owners had taken over the inn. Nothing seemed like it had changed much, but I'd only just arrived and couldn't be sure.

Looking to my left, I saw the dining room still

looked the same, which made me happy since I usually spent a lot of time there if not in my room. All the dark mahogany wood glowed as if it had been freshly polished, and the delicious smell of food wafted through the air.

My travel agent had promised things would be the same as usual, and it looked like she'd been right. I crossed my fingers in hopes that it would be the wonderfully relaxing experience I'd grown accustomed to there.

I stopped at the check-in desk and smiled to myself as I glanced around. Whether new people owned it or not, The Gilford House Inn had been kept the same way it had always looked, and I loved it. The same deep red carpet covered the floor, and the walls were just the right shade of eggshell white to soften the room while sun streamed in through the tall windows on the far wall.

The inn had a coziness to it that always made me smile, like climbing into bed on a chilly day always felt to me. The accents and railings were all cherry mahogany wood. It was clear as day that a woman had designed the place. A man would have filled it with harsher colors like silver and black instead of the warm and welcoming colors of nature that wrapped you in their embrace as you entered.

I liked that.

If I wanted to stay at a cold and stark looking hotel on my vacation, I could have had my pick of any of the big names in the area, but that wasn't for me. I wanted some real personality and love in my vacation home away from home.

The young woman at the desk smiled at me and checked me in before giving me the familiar Gilford House Inn speech about times the food would be served and the various activities I could enjoy on the grounds or in town before sending me on my way. It didn't matter how many times I'd heard it. I always liked that little speech. It ended with a sincere welcome to the place, and a small gift bag containing some pamphlets for local attractions and three maple leaf candies perfect for my sweet tooth.

I walked up the staircase on the other side of the dining room toward my third floor room. Pictures of the owner and her staff on the grounds doing various activities decorated the walls up the stairs. The pictures had been there as long as I could remember, and the one I liked the most featured the workers and her outside at a picnic with a large banner that said "Staff Appreciation Day" over the heads of everyone gathered for a group picture. Every person in the picture smiled warmly, and in the center stood a beaming woman being hugged by a few of the staff. Too many places didn't do that for their employees anymore, and I made a mental note to throw a party for my own staff soon. They deserved it, and it would probably be a blast, though I hoped someone else had better barbecuing skills than I did.

When I reached the third floor, nearby I heard a man berating a woman I could hear sniffling. I turned the corner and took in the scene before me. Like a child being scolded by an angry father, the maid trembled as she picked up sheets and towels scattered on the floor around her while the man barked at her.

"How hard is it to just do your damned job? Are you incapable of even the most basic tasks?"

"I didn't mean to mess up again, Mr. Gilford," the woman said quietly as she stood up, her arms full.

"Seriously? How hard can it be to simply walk into a room, deposit towels, wipe shit down, and walk the fuck back out again? You aren't even the only cleaner. Your only job is to pick up old towels and put new ones down and wipe some things, and you have a fucking co-worker helping you! A trained monkey could do your job with more efficiency and fewer tears!"

"I'm sorry...Mr..."

"Oh, here we go again with the I'm sorry business. Can you drop the crocodile tears act for a second and just listen? How is the entire second floor still out of towels? I've got people up my ass all morning about needing towels, and you're up here, a floor away, goofing off. Why?"

I stepped forward and put my hand up in front of the man's face. "Stop treating her like that," I said as I leaned my bags against the wall and bent down to help her pick up more of the linens.

The woman, whose name I assumed was Sue from her name tag, glanced at me with a grateful look in her eyes but she was obviously too scared to thank me given the wrath she was receiving from the jackass looming above the two of us.

"This is none of your business, lady. Go enjoy your stay elsewhere, if you don't mind," the man growled as I handed the woman the linens.

Standing up, I leveled my gaze on him and wondered who this rude man could be. This definitely was a change from what the inn had been when that lovely woman had owned it.

"I'm sorry. What's your name?" he asked, his eyes roaming from my face down my body and his tone dripping with sugary sweetness, even as how rude he had just been to the maid hung in the air around us.

Even his body language changed as he shifted his weight so his body faced me and let his arms fall to his sides in a less threatening and more flirtatious manner. It was a little stunning and quite unnerving to see someone switch drastic gears so quickly, and it was the furthest thing from attractive.

I pointed at his chest and said, "That's irrelevant. You know what is relevant? The fact that this woman doesn't deserve to be treated like dirt simply because her job is to make your bed and leave mints on where you rest your head."

Slowly, I saw a smile tug at the corners of the maid's mouth. The man shook his head angrily before barking at her, "Just get out of here. Try not to mess anything else up. Fix the towel situation and start wiping down the dining room when you're done. It looks filthy down there."

"Yes sir," she muttered before scurrying off.

He turned to speak to me, but I rolled my eyes and walked off towards my room, leaving him standing at the end of the hall looking like the jackass he'd just shown himself to be. I didn't glance back and instead turned the corner to my room.

As charming as my usual room on the floor below, the place I would spend the next few days and nights enveloped me in that lovely way only The Gilford House Inn could with its homey décor. The walls remained the warm tan color they'd always been, and beneath my feet was the dark hardwood floor with its imperfections and scratches I believed were original to the building.

A mahogany sleigh bed positioned on one of the room's long walls and the two cream colored Queen Anne chairs with a small table situated between them were the only pieces of furniture in the room, other than an armoire opposite the bed, but the room didn't feel empty, despite there being ample space to move around.

Settling in, I emptied my suitcase and put my clothes away before checking out the scenery from my window. Looking out, I admired the view of the mountainside as I struggled to enjoy it. Everything else about The Gilford House Inn had been pleasant, like always, but the uncomfortable scene I'd witnessed minutes earlier stayed with me.

The biggest reason why I'd always loved coming to the inn was the peaceful and positive atmosphere that greeted me every time. The place contained a warmth and genuineness that had kept me coming back every single time. I now worried that had all but disappeared with the death of the previous owner.

It was all just so disappointing, and I couldn't help but wonder who had taken over since clearly they weren't managing their staff well at all. The woman I had met would have never permitted anyone to speak so rudely to any of her staff or guests.

There was simply no need to talk to someone

like that in any circumstance, and especially not in public. I shuddered at the thought of anyone in their rooms hearing such nastiness going on and was disappointed that no one had come out to defend the poor girl except for me.

But it wasn't their responsibility to do that, so I couldn't fault the invisible strangers sharing the floor with me too much. I hated seeing someone get bullied and pushed around as I had seen in the hallway. Being a maid didn't mean you had to be treated like the dirt you cleaned up. Everyone deserved respect was a motto I had lived my life by, and it had gotten me far. That others like the awful man I'd had the displeasure of meeting couldn't even muster up a tiny bit of respect for others truly bothered me.

I changed into shorts and an old t-shirt I liked to wear to sleep and gazed out the window at the brightly colored leaves being tossed around by the wind. Was this trip to be my last to The Gilford House Inn? I hated to even think of it, but if what I had seen in the hallway was the new norm, I wanted no part of it. I could find that kind of treatment and behavior in the city.

Lost in thought, I climbed into the comfortable queen sized bed and closed my eyes, eager to push out of my mind the events I'd witnessed. I let out a small sigh and settled my head onto the pillow, hoping the next day would be a vast improvement.

CHAPTER FOUR

Zane

FOR THE PAST four years, every morning I woke up to a sexy woman in my bed and the sun shining through the windows in my bedroom. Now I woke to a room the average grandmother would have considered a bit much and an empty bed that was barely illuminated thanks to the near constant grey sky that seemed to exist above the inn. Worst of all, I woke up every day to someone pounding on my damn door needing something. It was awful.

As I heard the irritating knock this morning, I sighed and got up to answer the door and ream out the person on the other side of it.

"Yes?" I said as a short and exceptionally pregnant looking Asian woman trembled before me.

"Sir, the kitchen shipment came in, and they need you to sign for it. I'm sorry."

I rolled my eyes and shut the door before

yelling back at her, "I'll be down when I'm down. He can wait."

It had been a month since my mother's lawyer had given me the news that instead of just getting my inheritance that I'd have to run this damn place for a year, and I didn't know how I was going to make it for another eleven months.

Scrubbing the sleep from my face, I stared into the mirror and wished for time to fly by so I could return to my life out west. I slipped on a pair of pants and yesterday's shirt and ran my fingers through my hair before going downstairs to sign the paper the delivery guy had for me.

"Mondays, right?" he said, his tone far more chipper than it needed to be for seven in the morning.

"Yeah," I grunted before putting the paper in his hands and walking away.

I left the kitchen to look at the dining room. Each table was set up and ready for breakfast, but other than that, it looked like any other restaurant before the customers arrived. Not that I gave much of a damn about dishes and what color the tablecloths should be.

I grabbed some eggs and bacon from the buffet and took a seat at what had become my usual table in the corner. Halfway through my meal I could feel someone behind me, and I turned around slowly as I rolled my eyes.

"What is it, Sue? Did you manage to ruin yet another load of linens?" I asked, my mouth still full of food as she stood wide-eyed staring at me.

"No...no, sir. I...I just..."

"What is it, Sue? Just spit it out. I'm trying to eat here."

"I just...I needed to ask if I can have a day off next month," she said, annoying me with every syllable.

"Why do you need a day off next month?" I asked before taking a long drink of coffee.

"Well...I have this wedding..." she answered before looking down at the floor.

"You know what, Sue. I couldn't care less about what you do in your personal life. If you want the day off, talk to that old lady Kathy. She makes the schedule for the help."

"Yes sir...it's just she told me to explain it to you and..."

My breakfast ruined, I pushed the plate away and tried to pretend that I didn't want to just get up and walk away from this conversation. "Just talk to Kathy, okay? Tell her I don't care why you have to have the day off."

She nodded, and with her lip quivering, ran away as fast as she could from me. Good. That was how I liked it. Every time one of the workers talked to me it felt like a migraine shot directly from my left eye straight to the back of my head.

Fuck, it was going to be a long eleven months.

I stood up from my breakfast, leaving the dishes behind, and headed to the back office to tackle the mountain of never-ending paperwork waiting for me on my desk. When I got there, one of the kitchen staff, a woman whose name escaped me at that moment, stood waiting for me. A homely thing, she had eyes that resembled a bug's and always looked like someone had just shocked the hell out of her. Thankfully, we kept her in the back of the house.

"Yes? What do you need?" I asked as I unlocked the office, pushing past her to take a seat in the uncomfortable office chair I kept meaning to replace.

She looked around nervously and said, "Uh, Mr. Gilford, I'm sorry to be a bother, but I have to go home early today and won't be able to make it in for the next week."

I let out a heavy sigh. Without her, I'd have to probably help out in the kitchen over the weekend, something I definitely did not want to do.

"Are you sick?" I asked, not looking up from my computer as I mentally ran through the list of who I could call in to replace yet another lazy worker.

"No sir. I just, I have to go home. It's personal," she squeaked out.

For once, I wished I had one worker who could speak in a voice audible to the human ear. I looked at her, disgusted. "Listen, Nicole…"

"It's Noel."

"Noel, whatever. I don't really care what personal issues you have. Leave them at the door when you come to work. When you're here, you're here. I can't give you the time off so suddenly."

"But, sir, I…"

"In the future, if you want days off, you need to schedule them in advance. Maybe my mother would just let anyone walk all over her here, but she's gone, and I'm the boss now, so get it straight."

Just like the employee earlier, her lip started to tremble as she stared at me, her huge bug-like eyes filling with tears.

"Oh, come on now. What is with you weepy people in this place? It's Vermont. I thought you guys were hardy. How can I get anything done with people crying all over the damned place?"

"Sir, I really need the time off because…"

I angrily kicked a box to my left, wishing she'd just shut up and leave me alone. "Because what, Noel? Because you don't respect your position here and the kindness it took not to clean house when I took this dump over? If you don't want to work, maybe you don't need to work here anymore. How about that?"

The people in the storeroom next to us watched me dress the girl down, but I didn't care what the staff thought of me. If they wanted to leave, they were more than welcome to. Hiring new people who I liked may actually be a blessing.

"Sir, my father is sick, and I need to go travel to see him. I know you hate when people cry so I didn't want to get into it, but they don't think he'll…they don't think he'll make it."

With my hand on the door, I let out an enormous sigh and shook my head. "Fine. You're not fired. Just get out and let Kathy know when you'll be back."

I closed the door behind her after she left and sat back in my chair. Shaking off the exchange, I dove into the paperwork I loathed as much as the staff.

I'd always thought that even if she'd invested too much time and effort into the inn, my mother at least ran a tight ship. It certainly didn't seem that way to me now. After an hour in the cave, as I'd come to call it after too many hours spent in that musky room filling out paperwork, I walked out to check on the guests. It was an effort being nice to them sometimes, but I needed to keep the place running as well as it had with my mother for just a year, so it was a necessary evil.

Luckily, there wasn't much glad-handing to

be done. A group had decided to go on a nature walk. Old people and hipsters loved nature walks. The idea was bizarre to me. I could easily Google a picture of nature and sit my happy ass inside all day where the awful Vermont weather couldn't touch me.

I said hello to an old couple who barely heard me and ambled up to the check-in the desk at the front.

"Good morning, Mr. Gilford," the girl said stiffly as I approached her.

She was very young and hadn't been there as long as the others but had worked under my mother for the last two years of her life. I didn't think much of her as children generally annoyed me, and anyone under twenty-five was a child in my eyes.

"Morning. Is there something wrong?" I asked, noticing how she glared at me.

"What you did to Noel this morning was horrendous. Her father is dying, and you bullied her to tears like you do just about every other woman in this place."

Her rudeness surprised me. Taking a step back, I said, "You're implying I'm some kind of sexist?"

"No, the men hate you just as much because you treat them like garbage too," she said matter-of-factly.

"Listen here." I looked at her name tag and read the name Mandy written in black marker. "Mandy, you don't get to talk to your boss that way. If I remember correctly, this is your first job?"

"Yes, and if all bosses are like you, maybe I won't have a next one."

"No, you don't get to talk to me that way. I'm your boss, and that's all there is to it. Your job is to stand here with a smile plastered on your face and greet people as they come and go. You're the gatekeeper. I don't pay you to give me advice on how to treat my staff. If people cry, that's their problem, not mine. I haven't done anything that damned traumatizing. I gave Noel the time off, so everyone wins. As for you, learn to keep quiet and do your job."

I went to walk away, but to my immense surprise the girl felt like talking back. "Mr. Gilford, with all due respect, which is very little, you're a bully, and your mother would be disappointed if she could see what you have become."

Shock settled into me as she took a deep breath to continue.

"That wonderful woman was full of warmth and kindness. I can't see how she raised such a hateful man. While I appreciate this job and will do it well, you don't get to bully me around while

I do it. You should start being nicer since we're the ones who bust our asses for this place while you get drunk in your room. What if your mother saw you treat us like this? How would she feel?"

I didn't feel like listening to any more chastising from the mouths of babes, so I stormed off to my room, slamming the door behind me. Looking at the clock on the nightstand, I saw it wasn't even eleven in the morning.

Christ. Disgusted, I sat down and pulled out my cell phone, looking at the picture of my beautiful girlfriend back in California before hitting the SEND button to call her.

"Hello?" she said after a few rings.

"Hey, babe. You watching over Cali for me?" I asked as I reclined back onto the bed and closed my eyes. At the very least having someone to talk to who wasn't in godforsaken Vermont might make me feel better.

"Hey, Zane, we should talk," she said, the tone in her voice sounding hesitant and cautious.

"Listen, Stacey. I know this long distance thing sucks, but I'll be back in California before you know it and we can get right back to where we left off. Your clothes being all over my floor and you naked under me seems like a good place to start," I said, wishing so badly that I could have her there on top of me at that very moment.

"Zane, stop. This isn't working, and you

know it."

My mouth fell open, but I did my best to salvage the conversation. "Babe, it's only been a month. I know it isn't ideal, but I'm going to come out of this with a ton of money. I hate it too, but if you just hang in there, I know we can make it work. How about I fly you out here for a week, and we can make fun of this boring town together?"

She sighed and the phone fell silent, but in the background I could hear someone speaking. A man. "Is someone there with you, Stace?"

"Zane, I didn't want you to find out like this."

"Are you kidding me?" I said, slamming my hand down on my bedside table as I jumped up, anger tearing through me.

The walls of my room felt like they were closing in on me, and my head spun from the realization that my girlfriend was there in the apartment we shared together with another man. I'd barely been gone a month, for fuck's sake!

"I'm sorry, I just…"

"You just what? Moved the fuck on already? It's been a fucking month, Stacey. I'm not some soldier at war and gone for years, for Christ's sake."

"Zane, I have to go to work. We can talk about this later."

"Fuck later. Go have fun with your new

boyfriend."

I ended the call and threw my phone across the room where it landed in a pile of clothes I had yet to get around to washing. In just a single month, my whole life had unraveled. I hated the inn and everyone in it, and I wanted to be back in my apartment in California by the beach.

And now, my girlfriend had decided to leave me after just a month for some guy. It was probably that sleepy-eyed club owner she knew. He was always hanging around looking for an in with her.

I guess I had given it to him.

For the first time in my life, I was all alone, and it didn't feel good. In fact, it felt like shit. I let out a big sigh and fell back onto the bed, wanting to sleep away the next eleven months and hoping that something, anything, could make them better than the first one had been.

CHAPTER FIVE

Becca

THE SUNLIGHT STREAMING through my window roused me from my sleep, urging me to get up and enjoy the first full day of my vacation. It was one of those crisp and cool autumn days where the clear blue sky and the sun beaming down gave the impression that it could have been eighty degrees outside, but a touch on the window told me it was probably perfect sweater weather.

I smiled with anticipation as I envisioned the day I would enjoy wandering through the woods. One of the best things about getting away to this place was the chance it afforded me to shed all the stress of the city and simply immerse myself in the quiet of nature. A nice long hike would do me a world of good. Maybe I'd even have a picnic outside on the front porch when I returned.

Before long, however, I came crashing back to reality when I opened my email and saw a message from my attorney letting me know that he would be calling me around ten to discuss the issue with my ex-husband, Dustin. I mentally kicked myself for not specifying to him that I should be left alone during my vacation, but it was important and probably shouldn't be put off until I got back to the city. Still, I didn't like being mired down with such hassles on my relaxing vacation.

A glance at the clock told me it was only nine, so with a lot on my mind I grabbed a shower, got dressed for the day, and made my way to the breakfast buffet in the dining room downstairs. As I sat picking at my eggs and bacon, I let out a heavy sigh. In truth, I wanted to let out a scream and pound my fists in frustration, but it wasn't exactly the thing to do in the middle of a quaint bed and breakfast, or anywhere else, for that matter.

Dustin and I had divorced three years ago, but he was still as big a thorn in my side as ever. All I had ever wished for when he and I broke up was to be left alone to carry on and live my life happily, but it seemed Dustin would have none of that.

Right before we married, I found the most incredible townhouse on the Upper West Side, and we picked it up for a steal. Three bedrooms, two baths, and an office for me, but even more, the townhouse became my sanctuary in the middle of the hustle and bustle of the city.

When we divorced, Dustin claimed he didn't care about the townhouse and agreed it was mine. After all, he was a new bachelor on the prowl after a few years of a failed marriage and had no interest in the townhouse we'd shared as a couple. Dustin hadn't even bothered to help decorate the place when he lived there, so he obviously had no interest in keeping it.

Now years later, he found himself some gold digging floozy who liked to live well above her means, and he needed money. So, of course, he wanted to sell the townhouse where I lived and had been living for years so that he could finance her expensive and completely gaudy taste. Even more importantly, he wanted to buy a new place for the two of them but wouldn't be able to afford the down payment without the money we'd get from selling my home.

I shook my head, not wanting to stroll down memory lane anymore, and finished my breakfast before walking towards the stairs to return to my room. If my attorney was going to be calling, that needed to happen in private, but I certainly wasn't going to ruin my time in the woods with a conversation like that.

As I walked past the stairs, the young brunette at the front desk waved and said, "Have a wonderful morning, Ms. Fox. Is there anything we at The Gilford House Inn can do for you today?"

She was so chipper, but I heard a genuine sincerity in her voice that charmed me instantly. If I hadn't been so distracted, I would have said more, but I just smiled and replied, "No, but thank you so much. I'll let you know if there is. Have a wonderful day."

"And the same to you!" she called back with a smile.

At least my stay at the inn was looking better than it had the day before.

I returned to my room and caught up on some work and a little social media before my phone rang at precisely ten o'clock. Attorney Edward Wickers was nothing if not punctual. I answered it and reclined back on my bed. If I had to get stressful news, at least I could be comfortable while doing so.

"Good morning, Edward. What are the chances you're calling me with good news today?" I asked, more hopeful than I should have been.

"Highly unlikely, unless your idea of good news is an ex-husband full of hassles."

Edward had a no-nonsense style which made him often come off as a bit terse if you didn't know him. I did know him, though, and I knew he wasn't a bad guy. Just someone who wanted to get the job done right and quickly. I appreciated that in a lawyer I was paying so handsomely.

"Good morning, Rebecca. I'm not going to sugar coat it for you. It isn't great. Dustin didn't seem to have much of a case in the beginning, but the fact that you have always earned more than him doesn't help. I know his attorney, Loretta Michaels. She's damn good at what she does, and quite the pain in the ass. Pardon my French."

"What about the fact that when we divorced three years ago, he signed the paperwork that left the house to me?" I asked, still desperately hoping that fact would save me from the nightmare situation I had been in with all of Dustin's crap.

"It's a big help. I can say that much. But honestly, it's not enough. He's claiming that you coerced him into signing with the threat that he wouldn't receive alimony if he didn't."

I pinched the bridge of my nose trying to dispel the headache forming just above my eyes. Dustin's refusal to act like a goddamned adult made me want to scream up at the ceiling.

Sighing, I stood to pace and said, "That's ridiculous. He declined alimony payments and took a lump sum. You know that, right?"

"I do. I drew up the paperwork myself all those years ago. It doesn't look good at the moment, seeing as he did pay for some of that property as well, but I assure you I am doing my best."

"I know. You always do. That's why you're the best."

My flattery never fazed him, though, and he simply pressed on with our conversation.

"In the meantime, see if you can smooth things over with him without involving his lawyer. Trust me. You do not want to deal with her."

Crestfallen, I stopped my pacing at the window and looked out, trying to stay positive and in vacation mode. All I wanted was some good news, but it seemed like Dustin was constantly gaining the upper hand somehow. The fact that he was a slime ball of a guy only made it worse. He didn't deserve to reap any more benefits from having been with me.

"Okay. I'll do my best. Anything else?"

"Yes. I have some things we need to go over and then I'll be out of your hair, so to speak."

We spent the next thirty minutes going over minute details that to me didn't seem to matter but I assumed were important if Edward wanted to discuss them. He wasn't the type for idle chit chat, so when he was finished, he abruptly said, "Okay, that's everything. I'll go over all of this and get back to you within the week. If you need anything from me, please call, and if you get any movement from Dustin in either direction, send me an email with the details. Didn't you mention you're on vacation?"

"Yes, a sort of sabbatical really. I needed to get away from New York for a little while."

"I see. Well, enjoy your time off, Rebecca. We'll speak soon."

Without a formal goodbye, he hung up. All the better really. I could only imagine the bill I had racked up talking to him for so long. I set the phone down and paced from the bed to the window as I worked to get over my anger at Dustin once again ruining something good in my life. I tried to relax as I walked around the room to clear my head, but it was no use. I couldn't shake the stress coursing through me, and I knew it was because I didn't want to talk to Dustin.

The last time we tried had actually been in person. I figured meeting for lunch could be more civil than a phone conversation, but I couldn't have been more wrong. From the moment he sat down at the table, things went downhill. He didn't want to hear a thing I said, and when I mentioned that I wouldn't let the townhouse go without a fight, he began barking orders at me that I'd have to, drawing attention from everyone in the restaurant around us and embarrassing me. From that moment on, I vowed I would do everything I could never to have to spend another moment around him.

But now I didn't have a choice. I had to speak to him if I wanted a chance at keeping my home.

With my stomach twisting into knots, I picked up my cell phone and dialed his number.

"Hello, Becca," he answered, sounding distant and uncharacteristically cool.

"Good morning, Dustin. How are you doing today?" I said, infusing my words with all the sweetness and charm I could muster.

In truth, it was easier for me to be nicer to the girl downstairs at the front desk than the man I'd shared a bed with for two and a half years.

"I'm fine. Just spoke to my attorney actually."

"Listen, Dustin, do we really need to do this? I know we've been curt with one another for nearly three years now, but what happened to the best friends we used to be? I'm not saying we need to return to that, but this whole back and forth over the townhouse is ridiculous, and we both know it."

"Becca, I don't think—"

I cut him off, hoping I could get a few more moments of sweetness in and control the conversation that would inevitably begin to go bad at any second. "Dustin, I love that place. You know that. It's my home. It's not just some townhouse. It's where my memories are. It's where we spent those years together. I know we aren't best friends, but that has to count for something. I don't want to lose my home, Dustin."

"Cut the crap, Becca. You and I both know that you can afford a new place."

And there was that nastiness in him that never failed to rear its ugly head. God, I hated him. What a selfish bastard.

"That's not the point, Dustin. The point is that—"

He cut me off and snapped, "That you're a spoiled brat who just wants to get her way?"

I sighed and shook my head. "I'm spoiled because I want to keep my home?" I asked as I paced the room, my stomach fully knotted up.

"Becca, I get that you want to keep the place, but we bought it together and—"

This time, I cut him off before he could tell any more lies. "Bought it together? You put up less than a fifth of the money, Dustin. You and I both know it was me who found that place and me who paid for the majority of it."

"Be that as it may, we owned it together, and I need money now, so you're just going to have to deal with it. Now if we can come to an agreement without the lawyers, maybe we can work something out for you."

I clenched my fist in anger and struggled not to whip the damned phone at the wall across from me. "Cut the patronizing bullshit, Dustin. I'm going to fight you tooth and nail on this. By the time I'm done with you, you'll be wishing you took the five hundred thousand I offered you. Fuck you and your gold digging bitch. That place is mine. Deal with it."

Before Dustin could get another word in, I pressed END and pitched the phone onto the bed. The nerve of that asshole to talk to me like he had any power over me or my home. If there was any justice in the world, he'd get hit by a bus on the way to his stupid attorney.

Needing some fresh air, I grabbed my jacket and marched down the stairs. The front desk clerk, the kind woman from earlier, tried to say hello but I brushed her off. I couldn't deal with talking to anyone at that moment and simply needed the fresh autumn chill to clear my head. I gave her a slight nod and hoped she understood before pushing out the front door and letting the cold air blast me in the face.

CHAPTER SIX

Zane

A N ALL-TOO-BRIEF NAP helped some of my anger from earlier ebb away, so I headed back down to the dining room. It was impossible to spend any real time in that bedroom anyway. With all the quaint bullshit my mother had left in that room I was stuck living in for a year, it was like living in a damned dollhouse. And if I stubbed my toe on that fucking green ottoman at the bottom of the bed one more time, I was going to punch a hole in those ugly blue and white wallpapered walls.

I took a seat at my table in the corner of the dining room and stared out the window at the woman from the day before, the one who confronted me in the hallway while I yelled at that maid. As I watched her, I had to admit she looked good. She paced back and forth through the trees, and each step she took made her hips sway back and forth. With every step, I was a little more mesmerized.

It didn't hurt that the only women I ever saw in the inn were old ladies or married moms, who although they loved flirting with me in the hallway weren't offering any real action. I hadn't seen a truly stunning woman like the one in front of me in what felt like an eternity.

She paced the courtyard in jeans tight enough that they could have been painted on and a sweater that perfectly fit her body. Idly, I thought to myself about how nice it would be to bend her over and peel those jeans off to reveal whatever panties she was wearing.

Or maybe she wasn't wearing any at all. Even better.

The top half wasn't bad either. She was a little smaller in the chest than I typically preferred, but nothing I couldn't work with. After all, not everyone could be as perfect as the California girls I had grown accustomed to. Granted, a majority of them out on the West Coast weren't real, but hell, who cared, right? As long as there was a handful I could be happy, even better if I had more to dive into.

I finished my sandwich and after a few more thoughts of burying my face and every other part of me in the woman outside, I decided to go chat her up. At the very least, talking to her might bring some happiness to my miserable day. It was better than sitting around inside that musty old inn. I was a red-blooded American male, and chatting some woman up was bound to be better than doing nothing, and if my luck with the ladies held up, I'd have her underneath me in my bed before the sun went down.

The bitter cold air hit me as soon as I walked outside, and I immediately regretted not bringing a coat as wind whipped its way through my shirt. My sweater was barely enough to fend off the chill of the Vermont afternoon, something my California blood hadn't yet gotten used to. My brain was still stuck in the mode that said if the sun was shining, then it must be warm out. Vermont was making a fool out of me over and over again.

"Why does everything about this state have to suck so much?" I mumbled, crossing my arms to conserve body heat as I hurried to catch up with her as she walked through the woods toward the small bridge over the stream that wound around the property.

Women always wanted to go there when they came to the inn. They'd take pictures on it with their friends and boyfriends, and all I could ever think of was the splinters I used to get trying to paint the fucking thing as a teenager. One time I got the wrong red from the store, and my mother nearly had an emotional breakdown saying visitors coming back from last year wouldn't think things were the same. Why everything had to stay the same, I had no idea.

Most of the inn was like that for me, memories of doing things I didn't want to after coming home from school. I didn't have fond memories of the place, except for the few times my mother and I had enjoyed a nice day together, but I could count those days on one hand. More often than not, she'd been too busy with the inn to see me and had just spoiled me with money instead of attention.

I shook away that thought and focused on the good looking woman in front of me, not wanting to let old memories get in the way of my favorite part of wooing a woman.

The chase.

"Hey! Hold up there!" I called out, but she ignored me.

Never one to tire of a good hunt, I called out again, "Hey! What's your name?" as I stepped onto the opposite side of the bridge from her.

Quickly, she spun around, and the stern look on her face told me she wasn't thrilled to see me.

"What?" she asked, practically snapping at me.

And at that moment, my past collided with the present, and I couldn't believe my eyes.

"Becca?"

Was it possible Becca Fox was standing there

in front of me after all this time? It had been years since the last time I saw her, but even though she looked a little older, she still made my heart skip a beat.

I could tell by the way she glared at me that she wasn't happy to see me, but it didn't matter. My interest had been piqued watching her walk away from me, and I wasn't the type to give up on something I wanted just because a woman caught a little attitude with me. Besides, I liked them feisty. There was something intensely sexy about a woman who put up a fight and made you work for it instead of giving it up so quickly. Easy women were around as far as the eye could see in California, and I'd quite literally had my fill of many of them.

Plus, I knew full well that beneath that angry façade existed a woman who knew how to please a man. Memories of our brief time together rushed through my mind.

Oh yeah. She definitely knew the ways to please a man.

"You're that guy berating that maid yesterday, aren't you?" she asked with all the disgust she could muster.

"I think we could at least be civil, Becca," I said, leaning against the bridge and silently cursing out the wind for its decision to start blowing its icy chill down my back at that very moment. It was a little hard to keep up the smooth act when I wanted to clutch my arms to my chest and shiver.

A look of recognition finally filled her eyes, and I waited for her to give me one of her beautiful smiles. I still thought of that way she lit up a room whenever she walked in. I took a step forward after she didn't respond and opened my mouth to say my name and that I was the owner of The Gilford House Inn, but she cut me off by putting her hand up.

"Whatever you're thinking of doing, don't bother. I'm not interested in whatever you're offering, Zane. I've had my fill of your type, thank you. I have zero interest in talking to you or anyone like you when I'm trying to enjoy a nice vacation. You already ruined yesterday. Don't you think you can butt out of today for me?" she said, anger dripping from every word.

She turned to walk away, but I'd had enough of people telling me who I was that day. I wasn't just some asshole, and I didn't need every single woman I spoke with to keep telling me I was.

"My type? You don't even know me anymore. You have no idea who I am these days. I could be the best guy in the world, but you want to judge me off of one bad moment from the hallway yesterday with a staff member who can't do her damned job, ever," I said, my tone rapidly shifting from flirty to fuck you.

Where did everyone get off being so nasty to me?

Becca stopped dead, and even that perfect ass in those jeans wasn't enough to keep a smile on my face when she stormed towards me until she was directly in front of me.

"I know you, Zane. You haven't changed a bit. You have too much of some things in life and not enough of others, and it's those other things that would make you a great person. That was always the case. As it is, you're obnoxious and cruel to others, and for that, I've got no time."

Angrily, I stood there with nothing to say. It was a stunning indictment and more than a little fucking rude if anyone asked me.

Which, of course, they hadn't.

All I had done was try to talk to her and be civil. There was no need for her to be such an utter bitch about it. I didn't stop her as she marched away off into the wooded area next to the inn, and when I finally shook myself out of my shock at being told off for the second time that day, she was about a hundred yards away.

But I wasn't going to let her talk to me like that and just walk way, so I ran after her to get my say in. Just like everything else about that damned place, she was all wrong. Just another one in a long line of people who felt like they could just judge me without taking even a minute to get to know who I was. She had no idea who the real me was now when I wasn't in a place I hated like that stupid inn. I was a good guy, and it seemed like everyone had just decided otherwise, no matter how nice I tried to be.

When I finally caught up with her, she refused to stop walking away, so I put a hand on her shoulder and spun her around to face me. Her look of surprise amused me for a moment before it turned to rage, but I didn't intend to leave without getting my say in.

"Hey, Becca, I don't know what made you so bitter, but nobody talks to me like that. You don't know me anymore or what I've been through. You assume you do, but you're way off. So how about this? Drop the shrew routine and talk to me like a normal adult does, okay? There's no need for you to go around treating people like garbage."

She looked me up and down, and for a moment I thought I had won, but then she set her jaw and said, "Way off, huh? So you aren't the same guy who left me high and dry nine years ago? The guy who I spent an entire summer with who just disappeared one day without even a goodbye? A wealthy, trust fund type who hates having to do this kind of menial work like dealing with blue collar workers and the unwashed masses? Let me guess. You took over this place when your mother died, and you're counting the days until you get to jet off to points unknown and leave this all behind. You'll jump in your Beemer and race off, never thinking of the people here or this inn again. Am I close?"

The truth sounded so much harsher coming out of her mouth than when I thought about what would happen after my year of imprisonment was up here. No doubt about it.

But I couldn't let her know that her words had stung. I took a step back, as I shook my head no, and replied, "I'm not that guy anymore, and this place is all I have left of my mother, other than memories."

Her mouth dropped open, and I knew I had won. Sure, using my dead mother as a pawn in an argument wasn't the nicest thing I had ever done, but there was no need for her to know that. Happy with getting the last word, I turned and strode off to the warmth of the inn I hated.

Even though I didn't like admitting it, Becca's words had hurt me. It irritated me to no end since it was rare that anyone got under my skin, nevermind some woman I didn't even know anymore. I tried to shake it off, but something about it stuck with me.

As I walked up the stairs and pushed open the front door to the inn, I had the same thought that

I'd had since the moment I'd found out I had to run the place. I didn't belong here. Nothing about it suited me, and I was constantly at odds with everything and everyone around me. I wanted to be in sunny California with a tan woman beneath me and a drink in my stomach, not shivering outside in the frigid air of the Vermont countryside being told once again how big a dick I could be.

The staff rushed around doing their jobs as I stood in the lobby. I had to admit I could never understand why my mother had never been able to accept the simple fact that I didn't belong there. Now that she wasn't alive, nothing was keeping me at the inn.

Well, that wasn't entirely true. I stood to inherit millions if I kept the inn the success my mother had left it. That's what kept me here. Not love for the place my mother had adored or anything to do with memories of her there.

I walked past the front desk and upstairs towards my room, believing for the first time that I didn't think I could do it. I didn't think I could keep the inn where it needed to be. It was one thing when I didn't want to do it, but for the first time since old man Worthington told me what I'd have to do for the next year to get my inheritance, I began to think I simply couldn't.

My mother and I hadn't been close, but to

deny that she had run the place well would have been too big a lie even for me to tell. It had been a long time since I felt like a failure, and I didn't relish the feeling at all. I was the type of guy who knew what he did well and kept to it. What was the point of doing something if I wasn't going to excel at it?

I moved through the rest of the day like a zombie, signing paperwork and barely listening when people spoke to me. By the time the sun set and I could retreat to my room, I felt only slightly better, but Becca stayed on my mind. I showered and flopped down on my bed and the thoughts of the time I had spent with her started rolling in.

She came toward me with a cute walk that was part flirty girl and part sexy woman, and I felt myself get hard just thinking about us together two nights ago. Becca Fox didn't come off like anyone who would have a one-night stand. Her eyes had an innocence to them I'd noticed from across the room at Candy's party. It was impossible to miss.

So when I succeeded in getting her into that tiny bedroom with me, no one could have been more surprised than me. The sex had been mind blowing, and for one of the first times ever, I wanted more than just that one time.

Becca stopped where I stood in front of the theater and smiled. "I half expected you not to show tonight, Zane."

"Why?" I asked, feigning surprise that she would say that.

To be honest, I was pretty damn amazed myself. When she suggested seeing a movie when I said I wanted to see her again, my first instinct was to say no. I didn't do the dating thing usually, but for Becca, I could make the effort because I knew the return would be worth it.

"Because you don't look like the movie type," she answered, arching one eyebrow suspiciously.

I had the sense she knew exactly the type I was but liked the idea of being with me anyway. Good girls always did. It was their fatal flaw.

Slipping my arm around her waist, I guided her toward the theater doors. "What kind of person doesn't like seeing a movie? I think maybe ax murderers don't, but I promise you I'm not an ax murderer. I don't even own an ax."

Both eyebrows moved up into her forehead, so I turned on the charm. "Not exactly the way I wanted to start out our date. Maybe we should start over." Stepping away from her, I held out my hand. "Hi, I'm Zane, and I promise to not mention any type of murderer again."

Becca rolled her eyes and shook my hand. "Hi, Zane. I'm Becca, and you never know. I might be an ax murderer. I think I saw an ax in the shed behind my house earlier this summer."

Damn, she had a way about her that made me wish I was the type of guy who could do the dating thing.

"Well, Becca, the possible ax murderer, let's do this movie. What are we seeing again?" I asked, holding the door open for her.

As she walked through, she said, "Les Mis."

I cringed at the movie title and told myself two hours of singing would be worth it.

Becca stayed silent as I held the door to my apartment open for her and she looked around at where I lived. The place certainly wasn't what I imagined she was used to. She probably lived in a nice white house with blue shutters and a picket fence to keep her cocker spaniel from running off. My apartment fit me perfectly, though, with its view of the beach from the balcony and a couple rooms so I could sleep, eat, and take a shower.

She headed directly for the glass doors that led to the balcony and smiled back at me when she saw what I got to see every day. "I'm impressed. This view is incredible."

I pretended like it wasn't a big deal, but I knew better. It was a big fucking deal. Nothing else about the place warranted the amount I paid each month to live there, but a million-dollar view was all worth it.

"Pretty nice, huh?" I said, sitting down on the

couch as she stared out at the Pacific Ocean below.

She nodded and took one last glance out the window. "Stunning. You're lucky to be able to live here. You must be some kind of trust fund baby or Silicon Valley tech guy to afford this place."

"Neither," I said, waving her over to where I sat. "Come here."

"Don't you have roommates who might come home?" she asked before biting her lip in that sexy way.

I shook my head and grinned. "Nope. This place is all mine."

As Becca walked over to the couch, she said, "It's all yours? What do you do to afford this place?"

Discussing how I paid for my apartment was the last thing I wanted to do. I had done the movie part of our date, and now I looked forward to the good part.

I pulled her down onto my lap and smiled up at her. "Talking about money is just boring. I'd rather talk about you, or even better, do something else with you."

Her dark eyes sparkled with interest at my mention of doing other things with her, so I slid my hand behind her head and pulled her down to my mouth. Her lips tasted like a mixture of sweet and salty from the licorice and popcorn she ate at the movies. Sliding my tongue into her mouth, I flicked the tip of it along the inside of her lips, loving the softness of them.

For as prim and proper as she seemed earlier, the woman who'd rocked my world just hours after we'd met the other night blossomed right in front of me, making my body come alive. I slid my hands down her back and squeezed her perfect ass in my hands, pulling her onto my cock.

She rocked in my lap, making me instantly hard, and then leaned back away from me. Looking down into my eyes, she asked in an innocent voice, "What are we doing, Zane?"

I lifted my hips off the couch and pressed my cock against the front of her jeans. "What we both want. A repeat of the other night."

Becca waited a moment before nodding and then kissed me again as she dragged her nails along the back of my neck. Her touch drove me wild, making me want her right at that moment. Unzipping her jeans, I slid my hand into the tight space between her clothes and her pussy, dying to be inside her in whatever way possible.

"Wait," she said on a moan before standing up and leaving me rock hard and aching for her to return.

In a second, she slid her jeans down her legs, followed by her underwear, leaving her naked from the waist down. My need to have her around my cock nearly overwhelmed me, so I quickly shed my clothes and slipped on a condom before I pulled her back onto my lap so her pussy was perfectly positioned to take all of me.

"Let me see you ride me, baby," I groaned.

She obliged without another word, easing herself down on my cock until we joined skin to skin, my hands holding her hips to keep her where she belonged. Like the first time, her body felt like it had been made to match mine. Tight and wet, she slid up and down my shaft, slowly inching me toward coming and then easing off at the exact moment to bring me back from the brink.

I dug my fingertips into her tender skin and moved her faster, eager to feel her come apart around me as I came hard. She stared down at me with a look that felt like she saw right through me.

"Oh, God…this feels so good," she moaned in a strangled voice.

With that, we began to move in tandem, me thrusting into her tight cunt and her riding my cock as we both raced toward that moment we craved. Our mouths devoured one another and our hands roamed our bodies, each of us eager to feel every inch of the other.

Once again, she rocked my world, and I had no idea why. She didn't really feel much different than any other female I'd slept with, but something about Becca got into my heart and made me care that she felt the pleasure I usually only sought for myself.

Her cunt tightened around my cock and seconds

later, she stopped moving and leaned forward to sink her teeth into my shoulder. A mixture of pleasure and pain as her body milked my cock and she bit into me made my head swim, and then I exploded into her with a low groan. We remained there, suspended in our mutual release for what seemed like forever, and then I exhaled and opened my eyes to see her sit up on me.

In a voice barely above a whisper, Becca said, "For the second time, I feel like I should tell you that I don't usually do this kind of thing."

The sweetness and vulnerability in her eyes charmed me, something no other woman had ever done before, and I wanted to make sure she didn't feel guilty about what we'd done. Incredible sex should never make anyone feel bad.

"Don't worry. I'm not judging."

My words made her frown, and she lowered her eyes, avoiding my gaze. "If I'm being honest, I've never done this before with anyone."

For a moment, I wondered if all the blood was still rushing away from my brain because of what we'd just done. Was she saying she had been a virgin until we got together that first night?

"What do you mean? Like…sex itself or…?"

She lifted her head and smiled sweetly. "Don't be silly. Of course I've had sex before. I've just never had sex with someone I wasn't involved in a relationship with."

"Oh."

I had no idea what to say to that. I didn't do relationships. Ever.

Well, never before.

An awkward silence settled in between us, and then she slid off my lap and stood up to get dressed. Without looking at me, she said, "I guess I better get going."

Something in me hated seeing her like that, so I quickly slid my pants on and stopped her as she began walking to the door. "You don't have to go right now, do you?"

I had no idea why I said that. I'd never asked a woman to stay after sleeping with her. But Becca Fox had something about her that made me want to know her more than just sex.

CHAPTER SEVEN

Becca

A DEEP RUMBLING in my stomach woke me up, so I hurriedly got myself presentable and then made my way towards the smell of salty bacon and eggs that wafted up from the dining room downstairs. Strangely, when I was back home, I never cared much for breakfast and often wouldn't eat my first meal until lunchtime at work, but whenever I was on vacation, I never missed breakfast.

My hands slid along the smooth banister as I headed down the stairs, and I once again smiled up at the pictures on the wall as I rushed to hit the breakfast buffet with vigor before sitting down to start my day. Like always, the food impressed, even though I chose the less fancy French toast and bacon instead of having the chef make me an omelet. Fellow diners enjoyed their food around me, content with their delicious meals.

As I finished the last of my bacon, I looked up

and saw Zane sitting at a table in the corner by the front facing window. The morning light shone on his face, and I could see he looked far away as he absentmindedly fed himself. His hair fell in his eyes in a way that told me he hadn't bothered to cut it in a while, and instead of sitting upright, he sat slouched and frowning. He looked depressed, and although part of me wondered if he deserved it for how awful he'd been to that maid the day I arrived, I was too good a person to take any joy in someone looking sad after losing his mother.

Something inside me stirred, and after a little while, I realized it was guilt. I felt terrible about what I had said the day before. Sure, Zane Gilford wasn't the best guy on the planet. Far from it, and I knew that from firsthand experience. But I had taken a lot of the anger I was feeling about my own personal problems out on him, and I didn't think he had exactly deserved that, especially since he had just gone through the death of his mother.

I'd always strived to be a woman who kept her emotions controlled instead of letting them overflow onto other people. Usually, I did it with ease. I pressed a smile onto my face when I needed to, and I kept people at arm's length so there was no opportunity for emotions and feelings to get in the way.

Cringing, I replayed yesterday in my mind.

After I'd realized the owner of the inn had been Zane's mother, I still responded to his attempt to speak to me by hurling insults in his face. I shouldn't have been so hard on him, even if he had deserved it a little bit because of how he'd acted.

But had he really done anything worse than hit on me on that bridge? Had he really deserved all that wrath, even with what had happened between us in the past? Wasn't the past just that, the past?

I tried to think of how I might have acted in the immediate aftermath of my mother passing away, and the thought brought tears to my eyes faster than I could even consider how I might act out over the situation. They were heavy questions to be debating so early in the day, but it wasn't like me to avoid them if they cropped up.

If his mother had been alive, it might have been a different story, but something made me feel like I needed to go over and apologize to him for my behavior. Maybe I felt like I owed it to his mother's memory. Surely a woman like that couldn't have raised a complete asshole.

The bus boy cleared my emptied plate, which I took as a sign it was time to go over to speak to Zane, so I stood up and straightened my sweater and jeans before taking a deep breath and turning toward where he sat. It felt like a long walk across the not so big dining room, and the entire way I tried planning out the words I would say to him. I didn't want to be too stern about anything and upset him, but I also didn't want my apology to just let him off the hook for being an asshole to his staff or me all that time ago.

Finally, I stopped near him, and I realized I didn't fully know what to say to Zane Gilford on a lot of subjects. I silently stood next to him and said in a tone barely more than a whisper, "Excuse me."

He responded by staring up at me blankly. There wasn't that typical cocky smile of his or even the grimace I'd seen him wear in the past two days. Hell, there wasn't even anger. Worse, there was nothing even resembling a real expression on his face, and somehow that made me sadder.

An uncomfortable silence hung between us until I said, "I...I just wanted to apologize for what I said yesterday. It was way out of line."

He narrowed his eyes as he continued to look up at me, but I felt like I needed to say more. "I was so sorry to hear about your mother. She was a very nice lady. I only had the chance to speak to her once on a visit here last year, but she loved this place and took such tender loving care of everything about it, and it showed. I shouldn't have said those things about you and this place.

You were right. I didn't know what I was saying."

To my relief, he gave me a small smile but continued to say nothing, only offering a nod. After a second, I had a sense he didn't want to talk and I'd said what was on my mind, so I returned his smile and said, "Well, I won't bother you anymore. I just wanted to say I was sorry about what I said and your mother's passing. She really was wonderful, and I know the staff all loved her very much. I'm happy to see you're keeping the place basically the same. She gave this place a lot of charm, and it hasn't faded, not even a little bit."

I wrung my hands for a moment before nodding and turning to walk away, but as I did, I heard him say, "She really did love this place. It's so strange to think of it existing without her."

Looking back at him, I sensed a sadness in his words and wondered if he wanted to talk about it. "It's a beautiful legacy of her life."

"Her favorite time was breakfast. It sounds strange, but it was. I was never much of an early riser as a kid, but she was always so jazzed to come down here and talk with all the guests. It's not my specialty, but breakfast is a nice time I guess. I've even tried talking to guests a few times, and they don't irritate me as much as the staff does, to be honest. Breakfast time is when I think of her the most. It was the one meal we'd share together whenever I came here."

I smiled to myself and turned back around. Maybe I had been wrong about Zane. Maybe there was still that side to him, a tender side that I'd known back in California. After all, someone who talked about their mother that way couldn't be the worst person on the planet.

I knew he wasn't that anyway. A jerk with commitment issues, sure, but not the worst guy on the planet. Hell, not even the worst guy I had ever encountered. Maybe, just maybe, he wasn't the horrible jackass I thought he was after all those years.

"Part of her will always be here as long as it's called The Gilford House Inn. Besides, who she was is infused in so much of this place. The colors alone make me think of her. She was wearing pink the day I met her, and she looked like part of the inn had sprung to life. I'm sure you really miss her."

He nodded and said in a soft voice, "I'm sorry we got off on the wrong foot, Becca."

And then he flashed me that exceptionally sexy smile I knew never failed to charm whoever received it. He was flirting with me. Damnit, I didn't like that one bit. He was using his mother's death as a way to hit on me. I didn't appreciate someone being so manipulative. How could it be that we had just been talking about his deceased mother and her favorite time of the day being breakfast, and then he slid into flirting so suddenly? I didn't have any dead parents, but I had a feeling if I did I wouldn't be trying to make a move on someone immediately after recalling fond memories of them.

Angry, my tone switched from sweet to serious in a flash as I answered, "Well, maybe you shouldn't berate your workers like you did with that poor woman. Maybe you wouldn't dislike them so much and they wouldn't hate you in return if you treated them with respect."

At the very least, maybe I could convince him to start treating the people who worked for him like people instead of animals to be pushed around. Zane grimaced and arched one of his eyebrows, clearly not liking how I'd changed the conversation.

"Well, maybe I can make it up to you with dinner. Tonight, say seven?"

God, he was slick! Too slick for my taste now.

I'd been wrong. There wasn't a decent side to him. Guys like Zane Gilford were a dime a dozen, especially in a city like New York, and I found myself repulsed by him.

How could someone be so slimy? His mother was barely in the grave, and he was using her death as a ploy to get me to go on a date with him. It was disgusting. It reminded me how when we were together, though it was only for a very brief time, he had a knack for getting me to do what he wanted. When I was younger, I'd had real trouble telling people, especially guys, no and would do whatever they wanted if they were slick enough.

And Zane had been the slickest of all.

I put on my best sweet smile and said, "You can make it up to the woman you barked at by treating her like she deserves. Even better, treat her better than she deserves since she has to deal with a boss like you. Have a good day, Zane."

Without waiting for him to get the last word in, I turned on my heels and walked away to go to my room, feeling pretty damn good about myself after putting him in his place. As I crossed the dining room, I became aware of the fact that a few of the staff wore large smiles and were directing them at me. I turned the corner towards the stairs and caught the eye of the front desk clerk, who smiled and gave me a big wink as I passed.

Clearly, they'd been waiting for someone to finally put the bossman in place. Glad to help, folks.

When I got to my room and closed the door, I couldn't help but smile too. It meant a lot to me that the staff had so clearly appreciated what I said and I had truly enjoyed giving Zane a piece of my mind. I hoped he hadn't seen any of them smiling, though, or there would certainly be hell to pay for them.

Flush from my mini-victory, I sat down at the small desk where I had my laptop, but I couldn't help my mind wandering to the first time I'd been with Zane. The first time I'd thought I'd been victorious with him.

Lying back, I closed my eyes as Zane slowly ran his fingers along the inside of my thigh, gently drumming them over my skin and driving me out of my mind. The noise from the party going on right outside the room we'd snuck off to faded into nothingness as his touch became everything in the world to me.

He leaned over me, and his warm breath danced over my neck as I kept my eyes shut, afraid if I opened them that I'd realize what I was doing and that I should run away. Zane Gilford was exactly the type of man I'd always avoided, and for good reason.

Everything about him made me want to surrender. His stunning looks. His incredible mouth. His beautiful body…

I knew all of this and still let myself be led into this room to be with him.

"Any chance you're a screamer?" he whispered in a deep voice before dragging his tongue across my collarbone. "Not that I have a problem with that, but all those people out there are going to know I'm

fucking you if you yell out."

Opening my eyes, I looked down my body and saw him grin wickedly up at me as he slid his hand up under my skirt. My eyes rolled back in my head with the first touch of his fingers to my drenched pussy.

"No...I'm not...not a screamer..." I moaned out as he slid a single finger inside me.

"Good. I won't hold back then," he said in a voice that sounded like this amused him.

I heard the sound of his zipper opening and then he was inside me, filling me up more than I expected. My breath caught in my chest with the first thrust of his cock, and then his mouth crushed against mine in a kiss that made my head swim.

He pumped into me, his hard body invading my much softer body, and grunted in my ear, "Fuck, you feel so good."

I scratched my nails down his back, feeling his muscles through his dress shirt and wishing I could touch his skin I imagined would feel so incredibly smooth against my palms. He pushed his hips forward, his cock plunging into my body with long strokes, and groaned, "God, I wish you were out of these clothes."

He sunk his fingers into my hips and changed up his movements to short stabs into my pussy that told me he was nearly finished. Something about knowing that made my body kick into overdrive, and

I arched my back to feel him press against my needy clit. I wanted to come from this rendezvous and enjoy it to the fullest because a woman like me never did things like this.

One night stands weren't part of my life. At least not until this moment in this dark room at the end of the hallway at a friend's house with Zane Gilford, a man who had pursued me from the minute he laid eyes on me hours ago.

"Oh, baby...that's it, baby," he moaned before stilling inside me.

My brain sent my body the message that if I didn't come in the next few seconds, he'd probably slide out of me since I didn't have the feeling he was the type of guy who thought much about a woman's orgasm. A second later, I wrapped my legs around his waist and pressed my heels into his back as my release tore through me.

Never before had I come that hard. I bucked against him with abandon, not caring how wild I appeared because I assumed I'd never see him again. The feeling was exquisite in its recklessness, and for the first time in my life, I didn't care.

I opened my eyes and saw Zane smiling down at me. "Damn, you are so fucking sexy."

As satisfaction settled into me, I chuckled at his comment. "Do you even know my name, Zane?"

His face twisted in a momentary grimace, a sure sign he didn't remember my name, even after talking to me for more than an hour. But after a few seconds, he smirked and said, "It's Becca. From now on, in fact, you're Becca, the first woman I've ever been with who made me want more."

"More, huh?" I said, stifling a full laugh at his attempt to still seduce me.

"Some women have it. Some don't. You do."

He slid his still hard cock out of my body and rolled off me, so I quickly pulled up my panties and straightened my skirt. Looking over, I saw him lying there, his pants still open and his cock out like he was in his natural element.

"You're quite the sweet talker. I thought guys like you stopped that kind of thing after you got what you wanted."

I stood up and buttoned my blouse before looking down at him. Smiling up at me, he said, "Guys like me? You mean guys who enjoy fucking beautiful women? And who's to say I don't want that again?"

"One night stands and fucking in someone's spare bedroom while a party is going on a few feet away isn't my usual style. I doubt you'd be interested in what I want, so I think we should just chalk this up to a good time and leave it at that."

Zane lifted himself up onto his elbows and let his gaze slide up my body until it met mine. "You don't know who I am, so maybe I would want what you want. At the very least, I want what we just did again."

Feeling suddenly awkward and vulnerable, I forced a smile and shook my head. "Thanks, Zane. It was great. I better get going now."

He didn't try to stop me. Instead, he merely lay there, his legs splayed open like the incredibly sexual creature he naturally was. The complete opposite of me, Becca Fox, a serious woman who preferred control to wild sex with a man she just met.

CHAPTER EIGHT

Zane

THE REST OF my breakfast didn't taste nearly as good as I wanted it to after that little lecture from Becca, courtesy of yet another person who considered it their goal to tell me how awful I was. Instead of the eggs and bacon filling me up as they should have, my meal just left me feeling empty.

And her words left me more than a little irritated. Who did Becca Fox think she was coming into my business and telling me how to run this damned place?

A single day without people jumping down my throat wasn't too much to ask for, was it? Was I really such a terrible person that everywhere I went people, mostly women, should be telling me what garbage I apparently was?

It should have been easy to dismiss Becca Fox's ideas about being nice to the help, but I couldn't do it. I wanted to simply blow her off and continue life as I had been, but something wouldn't let me. Her words stuck in my head, and no matter what I did to push them out, they remained.

By the afternoon after I had spoken to Becca, things began to unravel. During the lunchtime rush in the dining room, both the ovens decided to stop working on me along with two cooks who couldn't seem to get over their egos and admit that one of them had broken the damned things.

I stood in the inn's kitchen looking at the ovens in disgust that I had to deal with yet another problem in this fucking place while the two cooks sniped at one another like two Chef Boyardee divas. How my mother willingly stayed here for years baffled me.

"Maybe if you had set the timer correctly..." Tim mumbled under his breath as he glared at the far bigger man who stood opposite him on the other side of the oven.

Frank pointed his finger at him, his beefy face growing redder by the second and making me hope he didn't stroke out right there in front of me. He was on the chubbier side, so it wasn't out of the question. "It isn't a timer issue, you idiot. Did you even go to culinary school? Seriously, did McDonald's just give you a degree?"

"Yes, of course, master chef, because you're just rolling in Michelin stars, right? Please tell us all about the days of cooking for the Queen, you pretentious fuck!"

"One more time, Tim. Say one more damn thing, and I swear, pal..." Frank growled.

As if any of those words should set him off, Tim took a giant step toward his fellow chef and puffed his thin chest out. "What are you going to do? Be pretentious to me? Big fucking surprise there. And I am not your pal, so you can stuff it, you fat piece of shit!"

I stood in the kitchen trying to talk to the repairman who had come in to fix the ovens while those two argued like two high school girls. But instead of going off like I wanted to, I rubbed my temples and didn't blow up on anyone.

Damnit, I was trying. That had to count for something, right?

"Could you two do me a favor and take this out back? I don't care if you need to fight it out, but I can't hear myself think, nevermind what this guy needs to tell me, so take it somewhere else and cool the hell down," I said, keeping my tone as measured as I could as all the while I wanted to knock both of their goddamned heads together.

The cooks looked at me, surprised and clearly waiting for a bigger blowup, but I stayed cool. "I don't have the time for this. Seriously, get out. Take the rest of the day off while I hire a catering company to come clean up after your mess, and in the future, I don't give a flying rat's ass who broke things. Just don't."

"Sir…" Tim said quietly as if speaking louder than a whisper could set me off.

Ordinarily, it would have, but I was trying to be nicer. Seriously, I was trying, and these two were testing my patience.

"Just leave. Please," I said, struggling to keep my composure.

In truth, I wanted to bark at them until they both decided to quit so I could hire new people, but I was dedicated to making an effort. I wanted to prove Becca wrong. Why I even cared, I had no idea.

But I did.

I turned back to the repairman and took a deep breath. "Sorry about all that. I've got too many cooks, it seems. Please go on."

After pointing out a handful of areas of the oven I never knew existed until that very moment, he explained they both could be fixed by the next day. Resigned to the reality that I wouldn't have either oven for the rest of the day, I told him to do whatever he had to and called a local catering company to ensure the guests could eat.

It wasn't the end of the world. It would be fine. The catering company arrived quickly, happy to help quickly for a premium price, and only a handful of guests grumbled that the food that day hadn't tasted like the typical fare they expected at The Gilford House Inn. In the end, it was handled. Some guests seemed more than pleased with the food options, so I breathed a sigh of relief.

The next day, however, turned out to be worse.

"Mr. Gilford, the guests in the outer bungalows are reporting leaks in their bathrooms. Water's all over the place, and well, it isn't good," Mandy, the front desk clerk, said to me in a panicked tone as she held the phone to her chest, muffling our conversation from the person on the other end of the line.

I could still hear the angry guest screaming through the phone at her. I had barely finished my breakfast and was not in the mood for such bullshit, but it needed to be handled. I ran my hand through my hair and stared at the ceiling for a moment, wanting nothing more than to explode like the pipes in the bungalows, but I kept it in check and calmly took the phone from her hold.

"Hello? Who am I speaking to?" I asked in my nicest, sugar-sweet voice.

"You're speaking to Joseph Andrews in Bungalow 4. Who is this?" a man's voice barked.

"This is Zane Gilford, Mr. Andrews. I've just been told about the problem in your bungalow, and I'm happy to tell you that I'll have a plumber here in just a few minutes. He'll get this whole problem straightened out for you."

"Well, I should hope so! The water is dripping out of the wall, for God's sake! It's just not acceptable. Not acceptable, I tell you."

I imagined from the sound of Mr. Andrews's raspy and strained voice that he looked a lot like Humpty Dumpty—round, overweight, and dopey-faced. While that amused me slightly, it didn't help me deal with him.

"Mr. Andrews, I'm so sorry for the inconvenience this has caused you. I will be sure to see that your bill is adjusted to show today is on us at The Gilford House Inn. I'll make sure the plumber comes out to you first thing after he arrives."

"Thank you. We love coming to this place, and I have to say I'm pleased that you're following in your mother's footsteps, son. She'd be proud of how you're handling things here."

"Well, thank you for that, Mr. Andrews. I can only hope she's looking down at her beloved inn and seeing I'm trying to do right by her. If you'd like, we can move you to a different room, but unfortunately, there are no more bungalows, so the room would be here in the inn proper. Would you like me to do that?"

I knew full well that Mr. Andrews with his nearly-out-of-breath complaining didn't want to switch rooms. In fact, I suspected when I spoke to the plumber later that he'd tell me the water coming out of the wall was nothing much at all. But I intended on killing the current pain in my ass with kindness.

"Oh no, that's okay. I'm sure we'll be fine as soon as the plumber fixes things here."

"Very good, Mr. Andrews. And I hope you'll be joining us for dinner. The cooks are making something extra special today, and you won't want to miss it."

"We certainly will. Thank you, Zane."

"My pleasure, Mr. Andrews. Just hold tight there and the plumber will be out shortly."

I handed the phone to Mandy and rolled my eyes. "Hang it up, call the plumber, and tell me that Frank and Tim are in the kitchen."

Mandy's eyes opened wide, and she placed the phone on the desk. "They're here, yes. Should I get them for you?"

Holding my hand up, I shook my head. "No need. Just call the plumber and tell him he needs to get out here right now."

As she did as I ordered, I headed toward the kitchen. I found the two cooks hard at work preparing food for lunch. Poking my head in through the doorway, I said, "Gentlemen, better make dinner something pretty damn incredible. I have leaky pipes in the bungalows and other than sweet-talking the guests when they call to complain, I'm promising them a special dinner. So get to it and make the damn meal great so they forget they're fucking swimming in their rooms!"

Both of them stared at me with their mouths hanging open, but I didn't have time for their surprise. I turned on my heels and headed back out to the front desk with the desperate hope that Mandy had gotten that damn plumber to come out and soon.

Just as I reached her, she hung up the phone and smiled nervously, like she expected me to explode at any moment. "He said he'd be out in a few minutes. I told him it was an emergency."

"Thanks. Good job, Mandy. I'm going outside to head him off so I can direct him to the bungalows. If anything else breaks, floods, or becomes screwed up in any way, don't tell me. I don't want to know."

That wasn't a lie. I didn't want to know. I didn't want to deal with not one more fucking problem.

After meeting with the plumber and directing him to Bungalow 4, I walked up to my room and sat back on my bed with a grunt. It was turning out to be one hell of a week. Silently, I swore if one more thing went wrong, I would leave this place and forget that damn inheritance.

I hadn't realized I had fallen asleep until a

sharp knock on my door let me know that I was needed. I jumped up and opened it to see two of the maids staring at one another and me angrily.

"What is it?" I asked, feeling utterly defeated.

How was I supposed to put up with all this shit? They clearly were unhappy, and it was yet another stupid thing to deal with in my week of hell.

"I really hope this is important because I'm having a bad day, and the last thing I need right now is some high school drama from my staff, so make this quick."

"Sarah stole my tip," the one with the crazy curly brown hair said to me.

She had to be kidding. Didn't they have a supervisor they could take this shit to?

I looked at Sarah and waited, but she said nothing more, like just accusing someone of something in the most general terms was enough.

"Meagan's a liar. I didn't steal anything. I was in charge of the third floor, and the tip was left in 301. That means the tip is mine. It's pretty basic. If the room number begins with a three, then it isn't yours. Duh!" Sarah said, tilting her head back and forth like a bobblehead out of control.

I rolled my eyes, not wanting at all to be dealing with this kind of crap. The inn had a manager I had hired specifically to handle this kind of problem, but she was an older woman and was always calling off for one medical issue or another. Unfortunately, today was one of those days.

Still, she'd been a friend of my mothers, and I couldn't just fire someone for being a sick old lady. I wasn't that terrible.

Meagan shook her head angrily. "No, the third floor was mine today. You had the first and the outer bungalows."

"No one is in the outer bungalows since the pipes are all messed up! I had the third floor. Kathy said so."

I couldn't take it anymore. It was too much. I tried to push past them, but I barely made it into the hallway of the second floor where I stayed before they were following me and bickering like two spoiled children behind me.

"Mr. Gilford, she can't just take my money like that."

"It's not your money. Stop lying!"

"Are you kidding me? You can't talk to me…"

"I can do whatever I want, and you don't get to tell me what to do. He does!"

Something in my brain snapped, and I lost it. I turned around and roared at them, "Shut up! Shut up, both of you. Do you know how long this week has been for me? I've got a kitchen that doesn't work, a schedule no one seems to be able to follow, shit literally backed up in my bungalows, and guests who paid for them and can't stay there who think I'm their personal fucking concierge, and now you two can't seem to manage to figure out a simple tip dispute between the two of you. How is it I seem to employ the biggest fucking idiots on the planet at this godforsaken place? I'm so sick of this with you people. Figure it out yourselves. I can't imagine they tipped you that much anyway given how damned incompetent you are!"

I turned and walked back to my room, slamming the door behind me. I saw the clock read two o'clock. As good a time as any to start drinking. I didn't even grab myself a glass and opted instead just to start chugging the Jack Daniels straight from the bottle. I punched the bed frame, and something about the wave of pain that raced through my knuckles soothed me.

Tilting the bottle up, I let a mouthful of whisky roll down my throat and closed my eyes. Nothing I had changed about myself for the past couple days had mattered. This place still ran like a pig on fucking stilts, and it didn't matter what I did. Nothing would fix that.

I had tried. I really had. I'd kept my cool through all the bullshit that flew at me at warp speed, but somehow those bickering women behind me in the hallway had just set me off. Why couldn't they have just resolved such a minor issue between the two of them? Would they have acted that way with my mother? What magical touch did she have that kept everything running so smoothly?

The papers she left me offered some advice and mostly financial and legal information, but there hadn't been anything in there about how to manage these fucking people. I refused to coddle them, and I was beginning to think that was what she had been doing. Otherwise, why would they act that way? How hard was it to just settle a problem between themselves?

I punched the frame again, wishing none of this had ever been forced on me. I didn't want to be in this place. I didn't want to deal with idiot cooks who couldn't get past their pride and dumb help who couldn't figure out how to handle a simple fucking tip dispute or to not bring the dispute to me in the first place. My whole life had become one big mess bigger than the shit backed up in my bungalows, and every part of me wanted just to pack up and bail on it all.

The doilies on the bedside table flew off as I stood up and paced angrily past them and they somehow brought with them a new wave of anger. They were a perfect representation of this inn. Pretty and nice but ultimately useless. I wanted to go back to California. I wanted to be let out of that stupid deal.

After a few more swigs from the bottle, I lay back down on the bed and let a sense of defeat take me over. I hadn't wanted to blow up on the maids. Even worse, I had wanted to impress Becca with how I could treat my staff.

It hadn't worked, though. I'd been able to keep it together for a few issues, but what did it say about me that after just a few setbacks I ended up blowing up on people?

I didn't want to be that guy all the time, but none of them understood what I was going through. At the end of every day, the majority of them got to clock out and go to their normal lives, see their friends, and do things that they wanted to do. I couldn't remember the last meal I hadn't eaten in the dining room of the inn, and I certainly couldn't recall the last time I had been with anyone other than people I worked with.

Covering my eyes with my arm, I admitted the truth. I didn't want my name even associated with the place anymore. When people came to stay, they were expecting some warm and motherly woman at the front door waiting to give them a hug and a fresh baked blueberry muffin just for being there. I didn't even want to talk to them. They irritated me almost as much as the staff. I didn't want to keep being that person, but I was beginning to think it was just the man I was always going to be.

Maybe Becca was right. Maybe I couldn't be anything but all the bad parts of me. Maybe I was just an asshole like she clearly believed me to be.

Becca. She was a whole other issue. I had thought for a long time that I didn't care about her anymore and that any lingering feelings for her had disappeared. It seemed I'd been mistaken.

I smiled slightly to myself as I thought of one of the first days we spent together at the beach. It had been too cold to swim, but we had walked on the sand with our shoes off, talking like we'd known each other forever. When the water came up around our ankles, we ran back toward the beach and collapsed on the sand next to one another, laughing and out of breath.

I'd never been happier in my life.

She was beautiful. There was no denying that, but it was more than just physical beauty with Becca Fox. I'd never been a huge fan of intelligent women, and if I told the truth, she was probably too good for me, but I loved talking to her and listening to what she had to say.

The next day we'd eaten at some restaurant she'd adored that was all fifties throwbacks and retro with vinyl records decorating the walls and red Formica tabletops. She'd beamed as we'd walked in the door, and it seemed foolish, but when she'd taken my hand in hers as we followed the host to a booth, I had felt something powerful for her.

Something sweet that I'd never felt for any other woman. Like a feeling inside that I didn't want to be alone anymore.

I had genuinely tried to be better to the staff, mostly because I wanted her to know I was capable of doing so. I wanted to show her that no matter what I'd done in the past, I wasn't just the asshole she believed I was.

Word that I had exploded on the maids was sure to have already made its way around the building, but I couldn't do anything about it at that moment. Instead, I finished off the bottle and waited for whatever bullshit was sure to find me next in that damned inn.

CHAPTER NINE

Becca

A S ALWAYS WHEN I left The Gilford House Inn, I felt a certain wistfulness as I descended the stairs and smiled up at the familiar pictures around me on my way to the front desk. It was like saying goodbye to an old friend every time I left the inn, and I hated saying goodbye more and more each time.

I spent the morning quietly relaxing in my room one last time, along with enjoying one more luxurious bubble bath. I laid on my bed without making it, a treat I reserved only for vacation times, and had been perfectly lazy. It was a proper goodbye to a place that made me feel more relaxed and at ease than any other place I had ever been in.

Mandy, the young woman I'd seen every day that week at the desk, smiled at me and started the process of checking me out. "Did you enjoy your stay with us here at The Gilford House Inn,

Miss Fox?" she chirped.

I smiled politely and nodded as I answered, "I always do. I often feel more at home here than I do in my own home in the city."

"Are you from New England?"

"No, New York City."

"Oh, I'm sorry. It's just a lot of people who are city folks and come here are from Boston. It's a shorter drive than coming all the way from New York. Don't worry, though. I'm a Yankees fan!" she said a little too enthusiastically.

I chuckled and shook my head, waving her off. "No need to apologize. Between you, me, and the lamp post, I don't really watch baseball. Just don't go telling anyone from New York that. They'd have me shamed in the streets for even mentioning it. I can't even remember the last game I watched. Probably one my dad took me to as a kid. Now, James Fox, there's a Yankees fan for you. That being said, I am a proud New Yorker, baseball notwithstanding."

"Well, your secret is safe with me, Miss Fox. Once again, thank you for staying with us here at The Gilford House Inn. We look forward to having you come back and rejoin our little family soon. Is there anything else I can do for you before you go?"

"No, thank you, Mandy. I appreciate it," I said as I smiled and turned from the check-in desk, allowing the elderly couple behind me to approach and handle whatever business they needed to attend to.

I looked around and felt that same stirring of emotion that always came with the knowledge that I was returning to the real world. Being at the inn, even with the drama that had accompanied that trip, was always preferable to being back in the city.

A rush of emotion nearly overwhelmed me, and I looked around me, trying to take everything in just one more time before my gaze settled on the dining room. In the corner at his usual table, I saw Zane sitting there. It struck me that even when he was alone and had no one to impress or scold, he looked profoundly unhappy. I hated seeing someone look like that, even if I firmly believed that they brought some of it on themselves with their behavior, so I walked over to him and tapped him on the arm.

He turned to look at me, and his gaze went from the bag in my hand to my eyes. "Time to go?" he asked with a pang of sadness in his voice.

There wasn't a sexy gleam in his eye or the body language that said he was more interested in any other activity my mouth could engage in other than speaking. He didn't look me up and down and make me feel like he was having sex with me in his head.

I nodded. "Yeah. Time to get back to the nine-to-five rat race."

As I answered him, the sadness that had been in his voice reached his face, and he frowned. "Must be nice to get to go somewhere else. What did you end up doing in that rat race? Whatever it is, I bet you're kicking ass at it."

It was hard to see that much sadness on his face. Even though he wasn't always the kindest person, he was still human, and I hated to see anyone so forlorn. It wasn't often that I'd seen Zane Gilford of all individuals looking like a kicked puppy, but that was the feeling I got from him now.

I forced a smile and answered, "Advertising. It's not everyone's cup of tea, but it's given me everything I have. I actually enjoy it, to be honest. I'm good at it, so that helps."

There was an awkward pause as he sadly stared up at me, and I finally had to break it. "I hope things work out for you, Zane. You've got a great place here. I hope you can see that sometime. I think that when the day comes that you do realize that, you'll be much happier here and with yourself."

He didn't answer me, so with a final nod, I left him there at his table in the corner staring out into the dewy morning. As I walked out onto the front porch and let myself hazard a glance back at him through one of the side windows, I saw that his sadness hadn't been some kind of act or a way to get me to feel bad for him. He just sat there, staring out into the woods like a man who had lost his sense of purpose or direction. I hadn't often felt that way, but I knew what it was like to think that life didn't mean much. It made me feel even worse for him.

As I got into my car and drove way, The Gilford House Inn fading away in my rearview mirror, I couldn't shake the feeling of my own sadness that accompanied leaving that place. I didn't relish going back to the city, or my life, one bit. For all its ups and downs and the arguments with Zane, I enjoyed my time at the inn. I loved getting up late and having breakfast without rushing and watching the people who would join me for their morning retreat in the dining room. I liked walking through the woods and exploring my thoughts in a way I could never seem to do when I was in the city. More than anything, I enjoyed the sense of freedom that came from being there and away from all my troubles.

As I merged onto the highway and began the drive back to my real life, I realized I still had feelings for the bitter man in the mountains, feelings I hadn't acknowledged in a long time or had even thought existed. I didn't like admitting it to myself, but I had the urge to turn the car around and go back to the inn, calling sick into work for a few days, and seeing what I could do to get Zane out of his funk. I supposed it was the savior complex I'd always had when it came to men.

Besides, what could I do for Zane to help him if he wasn't interested in helping himself? I shrugged and drove on. If there was an answer that involved me, it wasn't one that I could find. Better to return to my life, however much that reality didn't really thrill me much anymore.

✧   ✧   ✧

LIFE BACK IN New York City was as it always had been, hectic and full of hassles both in my work and personal life. It was like the second I stepped out of my car and back into the city, all my problems came flooding back. Work became drudgery as I struggled with a nightmare client who seemed to fight me on every single idea that I had. Add to that the constant wondering how long I would get to stay living in my townhouse and the occasional calls from Dustin and I began to wish I had never left that wonderfully quaint inn on the mountain.

Weeks went by, and I found that every single day made me more and more miserable. Dustin never seemed to let up on hounding me about the townhouse. Usually, I could find my escape in my work. Unfortunately, even that didn't help anymore, though. I tried to bury myself in what I normally found to be a motivating and enjoyable work day, but every day just got worse and worse.

It got to the point where I felt like staying in bed all day, something I had never experienced before in my whole life. I had sincerely hoped that taking a week off to recharge my batteries would help, but it hadn't. Instead, I found myself longing to be back in the mountains, far away from the rat race I normally thrived on.

For the first time in my adult life, I was wholly and totally unhappy. I didn't know what to do. My mother suggested seeing a therapist, but that was always her answer for everything ever since she'd gotten hooked on those daytime talk shows that pander to people who should just get out of the house.

Night after night, I laid my head down on the pillow, hoping and praying that the next day would bring some shining light of happiness to my life. Hell, I would have even taken Dustin just deciding not to torture me with his calling about the townhouse. Unfortunately, day after day, I woke up disappointed.

Then one morning, I woke up to hear my phone ringing. I looked at the screen, surprised and strangely happy to see The Gilford House Inn number there.

"Hello?"

A male voice came through loud and clear, startling me for a moment. "Hey, Becca? I hope I didn't wake you," Zane Gilford said in an oddly polite tone I had rarely heard him adopt.

I sat up in bed and rubbed my eyes as who was speaking to me settled into my brain. "No, you're fine. I was awake anyway. What's going on?" I asked, confused and more than a little curious as to why he'd called me.

"Oh, okay. Everything is fine. I was actually interested in doing some advertising for the inn. I know you're based in New York City, so I was wondering if you could suggest a firm I could go through that would be good up here closer to me."

I thought about it for a minute, and while I knew of a few firms in Boston that could do a great job for the inn, I decided to offer my help instead. "My firm can do it, and I'd consider it a privilege. Consider it my way of honoring all the wonderful things your mother did for one of my favorite places in the world."

"That would be great, Becca. Thank you. Are you sure?"

"Yeah. I can come up there this weekend, and we can talk about all the details."

"It's okay. I can drive into the city. I am the

one hiring you, not the other way around," he said with a chuckle.

"No, better I come up there. It will give me a chance to get away."

"You were just here. You need to get away again?" he asked, sounding confused that I would want to leave the city for Vermont so soon after my last vacation.

"Well, you know how it is," I said offhandedly, hoping he didn't ask any more questions. I really didn't want to explain why someone who seemed to have it all in the greatest city in the world couldn't wait to leave it all behind, even if just for a weekend.

"Sure. Okay, this weekend sounds good. Do you need me to have anything for you when you get here?"

"A piece of that cherry pie your mother always seemed to have for dessert would be great," I said, smiling as I remembered the plump, sweet cherries and flaky crust of that delicious pie.

"I meant figures and details on any previous advertising done for the inn, but I can work on that pie too," Zane said with a smile in his voice.

"Good. I'll see you on Saturday morning. Can you get me a room, or should I make the reservation?"

"I got it. It's the least I can do for an advertising exec who's willing to drive out here to the hinterlands to meet with a client. See you Saturday, Becca."

We ended the call, and I couldn't help but smile. It wasn't the kind of project I had worked on in ages, but I figured it might be just what I needed to get out of my funk and get back to loving what I was good at. Something about doing advertising for big corporations felt so draining and impersonal. It would be great to do something for a small place, especially one I adored so much.

As I got dressed and ready for the day, I felt that happiness I'd wished for creeping up inside me, but was it the opportunity to get back to my professional roots or something else? Zane had sounded different on the phone. Gone was the miserable and disappointed man who hated his birthright, and in his place the person I spoke to seemed like the guy I'd known all those years ago.

I couldn't deny that for whatever reason, I liked the idea of Zane Gilford being genuinely happy. That I could help be part of that change in him made me wonder if he'd taken what I'd said to him about the inn and his staff seriously.

And if he did, why had he listened to my opinion at all?

CHAPTER TEN

Zane

O N SATURDAY MORNING, I paced back and forth across that ugly rug in my room while I waited for my meeting with Becca. I was very rarely nervous about seeing people and even more rarely nervous about how I looked, but with each pass by the mirror, I wondered if I should change my shirt from the blue one I'd chosen.

I didn't necessarily feel insecure, but I wanted to be someone more than the person she thought I was. I looked good, but I wanted to be more than that.

More than just an attractive outside like I'd always been.

Stopping in front of the mirror, I looked at the man in the reflection and saw what I'd always been. Dark brown hair, brown eyes, my mother's son.

And that was the problem, wasn't it? Zane Gilford, the spoiled son of Deidre Gilford was all

I'd ever been, so how could I expect to be something more now, even if I wanted to be for Becca?

I ran my hand through my hair and tried to dismiss those thoughts from my mind. I could be more than that person.

Pep talk finished, I walked downstairs and immediately was bombarded with employees in my face asking me questions as soon as I stepped foot into the lobby.

"Mr. Gilford, a man called today asking when you were planning on sending the payment for the repairs in the bungalows. What should I tell him?" Mandy asked.

"Mr. Gilford, I need next weekend off to go help my brother move. Is that okay?" one of the maids asked.

"Mr. Gilford, for the Saturday night meal, what should we be preparing for dinner? No one has sent me any menu, and as such, I have no idea what to order," Tim, one of my two diva cooks, asked.

Nothing like being met with a cacophony of questions the moment my feet hit the dark red carpeting. I suspected they thought I'd snap at them, but I needed to keep trying not to be that man.

Even if I wanted to walk right past all three people right out the front door.

In turn, I answered each of their questions. "Mandy, if he calls back, tell him I'll send the payment out tomorrow morning. If you need time off, talk to Kathy about scheduling or try to switch shifts with someone. As for dinner, I honestly don't know, so I'll leave it to your expert judgment. Cook what you want, Tim."

It may not have been the happiest version of myself, but it was certainly civil. I was trying, if not always succeeding, at making an effort at being the kind of owner The Gilford House Inn needed.

While they hurried off to do their jobs, I headed to my office to get ready for my meeting with Becca. I'd compiled all the data I could find on the inn going back for the past five years. Tapping the papers on the top of my small desk to straighten them, I wondered if my mother had ever thought of doing any advertising for her beloved inn. Somehow, without spending anything, she had been able to keep the hotel filled most months out of the year.

But now, I wanted to see if I could do better.

A knock on my office door pulled me out of my daydreaming about how my mother had built a successful business on little more than word of mouth, and I stood to open the door.

Mandy smiled at me and said, "Becca Fox is here. She's waiting at the front desk."

I grabbed the papers and headed out to see Becca standing in front of Mandy, the two of them talking like they knew each other. She looked good in a pair of black pants and a pink shirt that hugged her body perfectly. Suddenly, the last thing I wanted to do with her was talk advertising.

"Becca, thank you for making the trip. I truly appreciate it. Can we get you anything? I've got a cook or two around here somewhere who I'm sure would be happy to whip you up something."

She smiled and looked a little surprised at first before shaking her head. "No, no I'm fine, but thank you so much for offering. It's very sweet of you."

"I'm sure you'd like to relax after your drive, so what do you say to meeting up for dinner at seven?" I asked, changing plans and hoping this time she wouldn't say no to my offer.

She smiled and nodded. "Well, since it's for business, I don't see how I can say no."

"Seven o'clock it is then. I'll meet you right here," I said, my smile growing larger as I saw a look of confusion come across Becca's face.

"Why wouldn't we just meet right here in the dining room? What better spot to talk about how to advertise this wonderful place than right in the thick of things?" she asked.

"Because I've got another place in mine that I

think you'll love. I'll see you at seven, Becca."

I left her standing there with her key in hand, her mouth hanging open, and her eyes wide. Good. That's exactly what I wanted. She was curious, which was a good thing. The more Becca was unsure about what I wanted, the better.

A few steps away from my office just as two kitchen staff were about to scurry out of my way, I smiled and said, "Good afternoon guys. How's it going?"

They stared at me with confusion on their faces, but I just kept walking with a pep in my step to my office. It was just about lunchtime, so I decided to grab my food and head back to my desk, but as I spooned out a bowlful of macaroni and cheese from the buffet in the dining room, I saw one of the servers struggling with a stack of dishes as she tried to place them on the end of the buffet, so I took them from her and set them down myself.

"It's okay. I've got it."

She stared at me with her mouth hanging open just like Becca had a few minutes earlier, and I realized it felt kind of good to surprise my staff sometimes. As I walked away back toward my office, I heard her tell one of her coworkers, "He just took the dishes. Like he wasn't angry at all. He was…he was nice."

"No way. Mr. Gilford nice? Why?" the other

woman asked.

"I don't know. Do you think he's sick?"

"Maybe, I mean, he could be, I guess…"

"Let's just hope it lasts," I heard the girl I'd helped whisper, and I couldn't help but smile to myself. I hated admitting when other people were right, but it didn't feel terrible to be the guy no one hated for the moment.

A few hours later as I sat in my office finishing some work, I heard the fire alarm in the kitchen go off. I jumped up from my chair in a hurry and rushed into the kitchen to find black smoke billowing from a stove and guests rushing down the hallway toward the front door.

"Just what I need," I muttered to myself.

Not until the fire department arrived did I find out that Frank, the beefier half of the twin diva cooks, had started a grease fire. Luckily, there wasn't too much damage.

I stood on the front porch next to him in the chilly late October air as he began to grovel, and I shook my head. "Hey, no one was hurt. It's going to be fine. I just need you to be more careful next time."

He stared up at me like at any moment he'd break into tears and said, "Mr. Gilford, I promise it won't happen again. Please, just don't fire me."

I couldn't help but chuckle a little. "I think we've had enough fire for one day, Frank." I took a deep breath, still holding back the twinge of anger I'd kept bottled up inside me, and said, "Everyone makes mistakes. Just don't let it happen again. Got it?"

Frank had been cowering the whole time, nearly shaking in his boots, but when I let him know things were all right between us, he shook my hand and thanked me with a huge smile before everyone around us started going back in the building as the firemen gave us the all clear.

A small group of older women remained outside on the porch even after the word came that they could return to their rooms, so I made my way over to them and said with a smile, "It's all clear inside, so head on in and get yourself a warm cup of coffee or hot cocoa. It's the perfect thing on a chilly day."

The women smiled at me, and one of them said, "We love staying at this place. It's things like what you just said that keep up coming back year after year."

I didn't exactly know what she meant, so I simply nodded and smiled even broader. Each woman in turn told me that they loved the inn, and with each compliment, I just nodded.

The woman who first spoke to me patted me on the shoulder as she followed her friends inside. "Your mother would be proud of you, Zane. She always hoped you'd love this place like she did."

Alone, I looked out at the vivid reds, oranges, and yellows nature had colored the trees around the inn and thought of my mother for a moment, wondering if she would have been proud of me. I hadn't done much to honor her memory.

Not yet, but at moments like this when things at the inn didn't make me want to strangle someone, I wanted to prove to her that I was more than the spoiled son she died thinking I was.

✧　✧　✧

AT SEVEN O'CLOCK, I stood waiting at the front desk for Becca. As minute after minute ticked by, I wondered if she'd changed her mind and wasn't going to come to dinner with me after all. In all honesty, I couldn't have faulted her too much if she didn't show up. I hadn't always been good to her, after all.

Lost in thought as to what I'd do if she didn't show, I heard her voice as she said hi to one of the staff and turned around to see her walking towards me looking absolutely stunning in a little black dress and high heels to match. As usual, she didn't wear much jewelry, just a gold necklace and earrings. Some women looked great with diamonds and jewels dripping off them, but Becca had that natural beauty that didn't need anything gaudy. It wasn't her style.

"I'm sorry I'm late. I didn't know what kind of restaurant we'd be going to, so I wasn't sure what to wear."

I let my gaze slowly travel from her face down her body and smiled. "You look perfect, Becca."

She looked more than perfect. That little black dress accentuated her gorgeous legs and beautiful ass that gently swelled from her tiny waist. I'd always loved it when a woman's body was shapely.

"Thanks. You look pretty nice yourself," she said, beaming a smile.

"Ready for an incredible dinner?" I asked as I slid my hand down her back to guide her toward the front door, dying to cup that beautiful ass in my palm.

"And talking about what we can do to keep this wonderful place filled to capacity," she said, arching an eyebrow.

She wanted to talk business, and I wanted her. If I had my say, we'd both get what we wanted.

We headed out to my Mercedes, and as I opened the passenger door for her, I joked, "See? You were wrong about me. Not a Beemer at all. I've always been much more of a Mercedes guy. Beemers don't last as long, and the maintenance costs are out of this world."

She nodded as I helped her into the car and looked up at me with those big dark eyes I'd always loved. "Maybe I was wrong about you after all, Zane."

I smiled and shut the door, and as I walked around the back of my car, I couldn't help but feel like things were working finally. I'd gotten through a whole day and even a fire without losing my temper on my staff, and now I had Becca dressed to the nines in the passenger seat of my car. The only place better would have been in my bed, but a guy could wait for something so good. Now all I had to do was get her to fall for me again.

Sliding into the driver's seat, I glanced over at her and liked what I saw. Those legs went on for what seemed like miles, and it took me back to the days where they'd been wrapped around me.

If things went well, maybe I'd have that again that night. I could certainly imagine that dress being tossed aside as I laid her down on my bed. That would definitely make being at the inn a whole hell of a lot better. Really, anything would at that point, especially losing myself in a beautiful woman for a while.

We didn't speak much on the way to the restaurant, and that was fine by me. It just meant more time for me to reminisce about her being all over me. She came off all quiet and reserved, but I knew better.

Becca Fox, like any woman, liked to feel good

and I had something that would guarantee that feeling. It was hard to stay focused on the road while I thought about being with her again, and I couldn't help but wonder, was she thinking about our time together in the past too? She and I had rocked each other's worlds back then, and I'd only gotten better with time and practice.

If I got the chance, I'd show her how much better that night.

CHAPTER ELEVEN

Becca

ZANE'S EYES TWINKLED with a certain charm as he sat across from me in the restaurant he'd chosen, a dark and secluded place lit mostly by candlelight, and despite my best intentions, I felt myself begin to fall for him all over again. It was a slow kind of tumble, nothing like crashing in head first, but I could feel myself falling for Zane Gilford again all the same.

I didn't mean to, of course, and I silently reminded myself as I looked around the dining room full of candles that I was there for business, not pleasure. I didn't need to get involved with someone like Zane Gilford. I'd already done that and had my heart broken once.

The problem was the memory of all those nights I waited for him to come back had a hard time against the thought of just how sexy he looked sitting there across from me. When Mandy, the girl at the front desk, told me he'd been nicer to the staff, I felt like maybe I'd had some effect on him, but I couldn't just allow myself to forget how it had been the first time we were together. I'd ended up with a broken heart, and that wasn't something a woman just forgot about because a guy looked completely fuckable sitting across from her in a romantic restaurant.

No, I had to remember how important it was to just keep things business related and let that spark of interest die out on its own.

The waiter stopped at our table and looked down at Zane as he cradled a bottle of wine. "Sir, the Riesling you wanted."

My favorite wine. I couldn't help but be impressed that he remembered. The waiter poured us each a glass, and Zane held his up to offer a toast. "To the past and the present."

I looked at him and knew what he was doing. He'd always been so confident, and in our time apart, he hadn't changed.

"You remembered I liked Riesling. I'm surprised," I said as I lifted the glass to my lips and tasted the very pale white wine.

"You're the only person I've ever met that preferred German wine. That's hard to forget," he said with a smile.

None of that sounded true, but I didn't answer, in part because I wanted to believe he remembered my favorite type of wine for some sentimental reason and not because he was cocky and arrogant. I wasn't in the habit of lying to myself, but being around Zane made me think a little white lie about my favorite white wine wasn't so bad.

By the time the food came, I had drank enough wine to become more talkative, so as we enjoyed our dinner, I explained my ideas for how to let more people know about the inn. "I think when it comes to advertising, we need to focus on promoting the charm of the place. Anyone can promote themselves as a hotel, and there are other bed and breakfasts in the area that do just that. That's okay, but yours is such a grand old place, and the way it's situated on the top of the mountain is just breathtaking."

Zane nodded and smiled. "Sounds good."

Since he liked what he'd heard so far, I continued. "Some shots of the house with that valley in the background, preferably with some fall foliage, would be amazing. Even summer shots with a nice full and lush grove of trees would be great too. The place appeals to the older crowd but never doubt the buying power of those hipsters I know you have such disdain for. They love old, and they love quaint." I said, diving right in.

"What makes you think I don't like the hipsters I see all over this state?" he asked with a chuckle.

"Just the way you said that right there tells me I was right. I know you, Zane. That kind of glomming onto what other people made popular has always bothered you," I said, sure in my assessment of him.

For all his dislike for the state he currently lived in, he had a healthy streak of New England properness combined with the attitude of old money that ensured he'd dislike hipsters.

Zane nodded, but after a brief smile and a sip of his wine said, "We'll have plenty of time for that. I'm sure you're going to do a fantastic job, Becca, but for now, I want to know how life has been in New York. It's been a long time since we had a chance to talk."

I shook my head and wagged my finger playfully. "We need to talk about how we're going to promote the inn. Now to start, we also need some shots of that dining room. I love the pink and red hue to everything that your mother had for so long. It was like Valentine's Day all year in there. Did you change that, or did she change it?"

He scooped a forkful of sweet potatoes up off his plate and shrugged. "I don't know. I didn't change it. Maybe she got sick of one holiday all year long."

Undaunted by his sudden disinterest, I continued. "The front porch is another gem.

With the way it wraps around the entire house and with those adorable rocking chairs guests can sit in and look out at the woods nearby, it's simply stunning. I saw some kids playing with chalk on the sidewalk the last time I was here. That might be another good focal point. I think the whole appealing to families aspect is always good since sometimes parents can't just dump the kids somewhere."

He raised his hand and said, "Becca, if you don't stop working so hard all the time, you're going to miss this incredible meal and the great conversation we could be having. Tell me, how's the city? I miss living in one, and you're like a window to the outside world for me. I can't remember the last building I saw that was over five stories. It's like living in Amish country up here sometimes. The Wi-Fi went out for a few hours at the inn last week, and I swear, I damn near lost my mind."

I didn't know if it was the wine or the charm that hung off every word, but I didn't feel like fighting him, so I answered his question.

"New York is New York. It's busy, like always. They don't call it the city that never sleeps for no reason, you know. I own the advertising company now, though, so things have only gotten more hectic since I took over about four years ago."

His eyes widened as he nodded. "That's

K.M. SCOTT

impressive. So you were what, twenty-four when you took over?"

I chuckled. "You know full well how old I am. I was twenty-six, making me thirty now. Things got a lot crazier when I went through my divorce, but everything always works out somehow, right?" I said before taking another sip of wine.

Zane looked at me with a puzzled look on his face. "Divorced? You mean to tell me someone married you and messed it up? What an idiot."

I silently laughed to myself. Dustin certainly was a clown, but it didn't feel right to bash him in front of someone else who had never met him. Still, he was on the top of my shit list, and I didn't feel like complementing him either.

"Yes, Dustin wasn't exactly the perfect match I thought he was. Far from it, in fact. I think one of the biggest issues was that he didn't seem to be interested in having kids in the future, and I certainly am. There were other issues, as well. Don't get me wrong. Divorce was just the best way to go. I don't mind talking about it, but if you think you can keep getting me off track and off work, you're crazy."

Ignoring my attempt to steer him back toward talking about our working relationship, he frowned and said, "I'm sorry to hear you went through that, though. That couldn't have been much fun."

"I survived. So did he. Now, about the campaign—"

Zane cut me off before I had a chance to continue telling him my ideas for the inn's advertising. "I have to say, Becca, I'm very impressed. You own your own agency, and you managed to do it all in one of the toughest cities in the world. That's nothing to scoff at. Good for you. You deserve every bit of success that comes your way."

He raised his glass to me. "To all your hard work Becca."

Flattered, I touched my glass to his and took a drink, but something inside me felt hollow at that moment. It had nothing to do with Zane and everything to do with myself and how I had recently come to see my professional career. I'd become disenchanted with my life, even though I had spent such a long time convincing myself that everything I had was everything I'd wanted.

The townhouse, the career, the business, all of it was supposed to make me happy, but something was missing.

"You know, I thought working to get the brass ring was the important thing in life, but then I got it, and I found it meant there was always another ring right ahead. Not that it's a bad thing. I guess I just envy someone like you who gets to live their life in a place like the inn."

I finished with a small sigh as I glanced out the window at the quiet Vermont town around us before looking back at Zane as he shook his head.

"It's not everything it's cracked up to be. I'd give anything to be able to leave it all behind and head to the city where there are people doing things, creating things, and living lives that don't revolve around what season it is and what color the dining room should be decorated in."

"You have no idea how wonderful it looks to me. You get to run your own business and get to live outside the rat race. It sounds like the perfect combination to me."

He sat quietly for a few moments as we continued to eat our food before saying, "Well, tell me more about you, Becca. I want to know what goes on inside your head. You always had the most interesting thoughts of anyone I've ever met."

I shook my head and rolled my eyes. He was really laying it on thick, and it was starting to become more and more obvious that he considered our dinner a date, even though I considered it work. That's how it needed to be. It was one thing to get involved with a client, but a whole other thing to get involved with one who had already proven himself to be someone who could hurt me.

"Not now, Zane. We need to get back to

focusing on the inn. That is why I'm here, remember? I really think focusing on the rustic charm of The Gilford House Inn is your best bet. That's why people come and why they keep coming back."

"Becca, come on. We can talk about that later," he said with a wink. "Right now, I'm far more interested in you."

It wasn't as though I disliked being flirted with. Far from it. But his behavior was starting to get in the way of my work, and that simply wasn't something I would tolerate. That wink and the charming way he looked at me brought the memory of us together and the breakup rushing back to me, and I knew I had to stop him.

"Let me help you out, Zane. We did this once, and it didn't work out, so let's just keep this professional, and I think both of us will be much happier. Now, once again, I can really do a lot for the inn if given the opportunity, but you better be ready for record turnouts this coming summer season. I also think we should make a big push for your Christmas season as well. A whole line of promotion designed specifically to bring up the Christmas cheer of an inn tucked away in the cozy and snowy mountains of Vermont? It practically writes itself," I said, rattling off all the ideas I had formed on the drive up from the city and ignoring Zane when he tried to interrupt and interject with anything that wasn't work-related, which of course was all he wanted to do.

Finally, I had gotten through all of my ideas and took a deep breath before finishing up with, "Of course, I'll wait for your word on all of these things. You'll be in charge of final approval for any and all projects we work on related to the inn. I won't begin anything without your signed approval."

"Sounds great," he said, finishing the last of his meal and wine. "Now, let's get back to us."

I sighed and leaned back in my chair. The man was incorrigible, just like he'd always been, and I began to think nothing I said or did would stop him from coming after me, so I needed to give it to him straight.

"Zane," I said, taking a long drink and finishing off my own wine while he sat waiting for me to respond, staring at me with those deep brown eyes of his. "There is no us. I can't make that any clearer for you. I don't want to be overly harsh since I can see that you're really making an effort to be charming and sweet, but there isn't any us, and we need to get back to focusing on the task at hand, which is your inn."

I set my hands on my lap and waited for him to respond, silently swearing to myself that I was going to stand my ground. I never had with Zane Gilford on any other occasion, so this would be a first.

But an important first.

He smiled and leaned in a little closer. "But there can be, Becca. I'm not the person you knew before. Let me prove that to you. Let me show you that I'm not just some spoiled little boy. I know we got off on the wrong foot when you stayed here last month, but you caught me at a weird time in my life."

"And I am not as naïve as I used to be, Zane. Trust me on that. It's much better for both of us that we just keep things professional."

The look of confusion on Zane's face was almost comical as he answered, "I should remind you, Becca, I'm not the type of man who gives up when he finds what he wants. You know that from the first time we got together."

I let out a laugh as I pretended not to remember how insistently he pursued me when we first met. "Thanks for the warning."

THE WHOLE RIDE back to the inn, I tried to get him to focus on what the advertising campaign I had planned would look like, and he tried to get me to forget work and focus on what it would be like if we got together again. We were both stubborn people, so neither one of us intended to give in to the other person.

He stopped the car and turned it off before

shifting in his seat to face me. "What do you say to the two of us having a drink in my room?"

God, he was persistent! I had to give him that, but I had no intention of giving him anything else.

"Thank you for dinner, Zane. It was wonderful. I'm going to go to my room now and write up some more ideas I just thought of for the campaign. Do you want to meet again tomorrow around lunch to discuss everything?"

His mouth slowly inched up into a smile. "I like the idea of breakfast better. We can have it brought to my room and discuss things in bed."

"You never quit, do you?"

Shaking his head, he slid his tongue across his bottom lip. "No."

"No wonder your mother left the inn to you. She must have known your persistent streak would ensure the place continued to do well."

His expression screwed into a grimace at my mention of the inn, but I didn't give him a chance to reply before I opened the car door. "Thanks for a great dinner! See you for lunch tomorrow! You're going to love the ideas I have for you."

And with that, I left Zane sitting in his car wanting something I wouldn't give him. Not that part of me didn't want to. As much as my brain remembered what being with him felt like, my body remembered too and wished my heart would get on board so all of me could enjoy him again.

I closed the door to my room and took a deep breath. I'd successfully fended off Zane Gilford, and as I congratulated myself, I remembered all the reasons why it would be harder and harder each time to deny what my body already knew.

CHAPTER TWELVE

Zane

INSTEAD OF THE usual banging on my door to let me know of some damn problem, the sun slowly woke me, and I felt more awake and alive than I had in a long time. I sat up and glanced out the window and saw some deer running toward the valley off in the distance. One of them was a huge buck with antlers larger than I had seen before. He ran proudly through the trees and leaped further than any of the herd behind him. It wasn't often that I appreciated the majesty and beauty of nature, especially the likes of which could be seen at the inn, but I felt all kinds of different this morning.

As I got into the shower, I decided that I didn't care what it took to get Becca. I was going to win that woman over. Becca Fox simply needed to fall in love with me. I didn't care if it meant being different or what I had to change about myself. She would be mine, and when I decided I would have something or someone, it happened. Plain and simple.

I toweled myself off and shook the hair out of my eyes as I thought about her and what I needed to do to win her over. It would take some real effort, no doubt, but a woman like Becca was worth the time and effort. Hell, at least it would be a good way to make the months I had to spend at the inn go quicker.

Time at this place seemed to drag on, like I was in some kind of bizarre Twilight Zone episode or that movie Groundhog Day. Every day I woke up and walked downstairs, faced any number of ridiculous questions and issues from my staff, did work to keep the inn running, goofed off online for a while, drove into town to kill time, and then returned to do more of the same until I fell asleep at a time I would just be heading out back in California. Then the whole process repeated over and over again every day. If it hadn't been for the dates on the paperwork I had to complete every morning and the different activities scheduled for guests at the inn, I probably wouldn't have even been aware of what day it was anymore.

I sighed and closed my eyes. It felt like I'd been stuck at the inn for an eternity already, or at least for a year. I'd been all across the United States, and this was the one spot on the map where time seemed to stand still. I marked a day off the calendar I kept next to the small desk in my room and saw that it had only been two months.

"Fucking hell. Seriously?" I muttered to myself as I got dressed.

Two months? That meant I still had ten months left on the sentence I'd had imposed on me.

Well, at least I felt good about my new project. I had a ton of time on my hands, and instead of sitting around hating every second of it, I was going to use it to win over the woman I wanted. I'd always been good at finding ways to occupy my time like that, and Becca was definitely better than most of the things I'd gone after in my life.

As I walked down the stairs toward whatever nightmare awaited me, I looked at the pictures that hung on the walls for the first time. Not just glanced at them but really looked at who was in them and what they were doing. It was like going back in time with each step.

Some were pictures of the inn and the staff over the years, while others were of my mother and me. In every one she appeared in, she looked happy to be right where she was. I'd never felt that way a day I spent at this place.

I was a little boy in the ones closest to the

room I stayed in, my mother's former room, and by the time I reached the landing, the pictures were of me as a teenager. After that, all the pictures were of the people who worked at the inn. As soon as I could get away, I had and never looked back. I'd chosen to spend holidays at school whenever I could, and the day after graduation, I jumped in the car she'd given me and left for anywhere but there.

Standing on the landing, I stared at one of the last pictures taken of the two of us together. She sat outside near the edge of the woods in one of those uncomfortable Adirondack chairs wearing sunglasses and looking like one of those Hollywood actresses from the 1950s—poised and beautiful as she reclined in a white dress that showed off her long legs. I stood next to her looking awkward and irritated, a teenage boy with scruffy hair and gangly limbs who hadn't grown into his body yet but had more than enough attitude that came through loud and clear in my disgusted expression. I wanted to be anywhere else in the world than right there at that moment. She beamed a smile while I grimaced, an impatient, spoiled teenage boy.

As I looked at the scene captured for all time now, I cringed at my behavior. I'd call my mother and always wished her well, and she'd always be happy to hear my voice on the other end of the line. She'd never said it, but I knew I was a disappointment to her for not loving that inn like she did. I just never felt it. It represented everything I didn't want to be. I couldn't help but see how ironic my situation now was.

Walking down to the first floor, I saw Becca in the dining room eating and writing in that little notebook of hers. I had to admit all the ideas she had about the place did seem like they'd be great. She cared so much about the inn, and it was one of the things about her I couldn't understand. Becca Fox had the world on a string, and for some reason, she cared about this old relic.

To be honest, I didn't give a damn about advertising the place. I couldn't let it fall into ruin and disrepair or let business tank, but I really didn't care about making the place prosper any more than it needed to for me to receive my money.

But I cared about Becca Fox wanting me, so I'd advertise.

I pulled up a chair and sat down across from her, watching as she intently jotted notes in her notebook.

"Good morning, Becca. You're hard at work already, I see."

She looked up at me and smiled in that sweet way I loved. "Good morning to you too. Yes, I am. I woke up with a ton of ideas running through my mind, and I needed to get them down before I forgot any of them. Sleep well?"

Her interest about the inn was so genuine, something I didn't think I would ever be able to identify with. Then again, maybe she just loved her job.

"Always. I just wanted to come over and let you know that you have my full confidence as far as your abilities go with advertising for this place. Consider yourself as having free rein. I trust you."

Her eyes grew wide, and she set her pen down on the table. "Zane, while I appreciate that, this would work a lot better if you had some input in the process. You know this place better than anyone else here. I don't want to just take the reins and go off in a direction that you might not approve in the end."

No matter what she thought, I knew next to nothing about this place and really didn't want to know much more. "I trust you, Becca. You love this place more than I ever could. I know you'll do this right. Besides, what's the worst case scenario? It's not like you can run this place into the ground with a bunch of ideas for an advertising campaign that hasn't rolled out yet. If anyone's going to run this place into the ground, it's me, so don't worry so much. You'll do great."

My compliment made her blush, and her cheeks turned the sweetest shade of pink. "Thank you, Zane. I appreciate that a lot, though I don't believe that you're going to run this place into the ground. Not unless you decide to consciously."

"Well, I have a while more to do my worst."

Ignoring my move into how depressing my reality truly was, she smiled. "I really do love this place like you said. Something about it is just so special to me. I can't even put my finger on it. Maybe working through this campaign will do just that. I don't know. It just holds a very special place in my heart."

"I know it does. You're going to kick ass on this project." Touching her on the arm, I began to make my move. "I'm excited to see how it all comes out. So, what are you doing tonight? I know this nice restaurant in town by the movie theater. What do you think? Dinner and a movie with me?"

My suggestion was bold, and I knew it, but I had a goal and I intended on reaching it. She would be mine, come hell or high water.

"You know what? If I thought you weren't a selfish asshole, I'd consider it," she said in a tone that wasn't so much harsh but more bored with my asking her again.

The same smile she'd been wearing while I was complimenting her on her ability to run the campaign stayed, but beneath her words existed a dislike for who she truly believed I was that stung.

But there seemed to be light at the end of the tunnel.

"That's not a no. What's changed?" I asked, my cockiness returning.

If she wasn't saying no, maybe there was something there after all. With women like Becca Fox, and there weren't many, a no was a no, but anything else might still be a maybe.

Was there a chance after all? It seemed plausible. We had an intense time of it in the past, and those kinds of feelings were hard to let fall by the wayside completely.

Unfortunately, she didn't respond in exactly the way I hoped she would. Instead, she stood up, tossed her napkin on the table by her unfinished breakfast and said, "Nothing's changed. That's why we'll never be together. People don't change, Zane. It's a simple fact, as much as any of us wish it wasn't. I appreciate your confidence in me relating to our business together, but that doesn't mean I'm just going to run off into the sunset with you because of a few compliments. I meant what I said last night. There is no us, and you should really just stop trying to create it."

She left in a huff and walked outside, but I didn't follow her like the first time we'd argued at the inn. I didn't want a fight with Becca. I wanted the exact opposite.

I let her go and looked around the dining

room. Around me sat guests who had no inkling of what we'd been speaking about, lost in their own worlds, and servers and staff who avoided looking at me. Lately, I hadn't been as awful to them as I had been right after I got there, but the fear within them for me was still very much alive. They made an attempt to stay out of my way, and I sort of liked that.

Silently, I made a decision that I would never have made for any other woman I had ever encountered. I was going to be better, even different.

I was going to be the kind of man Becca wanted.

At first, my brain rebelled against the idea. It was stupid to try and change for someone. What she said was one hundred percent right. No one ever really changed.

But the way she said she'd think about going to dinner with me if she didn't think I was a selfish asshole before she walked out gave me the sense that if she saw that I could truly be different, she might consider being with me. Contrary to what many people thought of me, I was willing to work very hard for what I wanted. I just had to want it badly enough, and I wanted her bad.

The way she looked up at me when I came downstairs gave me the idea that something still existed between us, and not giving me an outright no gave me more hope than ever.

I stood up and walked to my office, making sure to not bother Becca with her walk or anything else she wanted. She would have complete control of the ad campaign and basically anything else she wanted in the inn. I would make sure of that. She'd want for nothing the entire time she was there, and the staff would be told to cater to her every need. They'd have no problem with it either since they liked her more than they ever could like me.

Resolved to figure out what I needed to do to get Becca back into my bed where she belonged, I headed out toward the front desk just as Mandy began to frantically wave her hand at me. "Mr. Gilford, there's a problem with the reservation system, and I need your help."

"Of course there is," I muttered to myself, diving back into the trenches of that damn inn where despite my best attempts, something was always going wrong.

No matter. This place wasn't going to get the best of me today because I had something more important to focus on.

CHAPTER THIRTEEN

Becca

O VER THE NEXT few days, I started to get a thorough understanding of what I wanted the ad campaign for The Gilford House Inn to look like, but I needed to fully observe the inn in its entirety for me to really pull off what I envisioned. Sure, it would have been easy to just use what I knew of the place, having stayed there many times, but I wanted to really give the inn something special.

At first, I wondered why I was so fascinated with the place, but every day when I walked down the stairs and saw Deidre Gilford in those pictures that lined the walls, it became a little clearer to me. The Gilford House Inn was more than just some random hotel in the woods. It was an escape, a place to get away to instead of from, and it meant something to the people who worked there. That care made it mean something to me.

I meandered around the inn and the grounds,

exploring little nooks and crannies I had never noticed before. On the main floor on the other side of the house from the dining room, I found a tiny room that looked like it had been a cloak room at one time. Unlike everywhere else in the inn, it hadn't been redecorated, so it had dark wood plank walls instead of the lighter colored painted walls found in the other public rooms. The space felt old and forgotten, but at the same time, it had a secret charm to it I felt privileged to experience.

Had Zane played in that room as a child? I imagined him hiding behind the wood counter with his toys, a secret place for him alone. The thought of that young boy in the pictures on the stairs playing here made me think of him as something more than that oversexed man I sometimes didn't like much.

Afterward, I headed outside to spend time on the porch, enjoying the beautiful fall scene it offered right in front of my eyes. The crisp air smelled earthy like leaves, and the scent of ripe apples from a freshly baked pie wafted out the front door each time it opened. Closing my eyes, I let the feel of the place wash over me and wanted the rest of the world to experience what I did there.

The warmth and coziness I'd never found anywhere else.

I focused on fully immersing myself in every part of the inn so that when I promoted it, I could do so authentically and without sounding like some cheap version of the truth. The Gilford House Inn deserved my best.

A couple days after my conversation with Zane, I stood on the far side of the dining room in an alcove that led to a small enclosed porch where people would take their food sometimes and saw a server drop a stack of dishes as she hastily tried to get too many of them into the kitchen. Zane come around the other corner, his eyes flashing anger, and I braced for the impact that was sure to be even worse than the sound of all the dishes falling. The poor girl frantically worked to clean up the mess, but I knew a mistake like that would enrage him. He stopped next to her and stared down at the broken dishes for a long moment. It felt like everyone around the dining room held their breath and waited for his inevitable explosion.

But it didn't happen.

He bent down and patted the young woman on the back before helping her pick up all the dishes he could while gesturing to someone with a smile to bring a broom over. The poor woman sat frozen on the spot, apologizing profusely.

"I'm so sorry, sir. I really am. Oh God, I didn't mean to drop the dishes. I swear. It's just that they got too heavy, and my arm slipped and...and..."

Zane stopped picking up the pieces of broken dishes and smiled at her. "It's fine. Accidents happen. This is why we have extra dishes."

With tears in her eyes, she whimpered, "I know, but I just don't want to make you angry."

He looked at her and shook his head. "I'm not angry. You don't need to worry."

"I promise it won't happen again, Mr. Gilford. I know this will come out of my pay, but I need this job," the girl said, her lip trembling as she struggled to hold back the tears.

I understood her fear. I'd seen Zane's wrath at the staff before, and I stood waiting with bated breath as Zane continued to react to the situation with a calm uncommon to him.

He simply smiled and shook his head before he finished helping her clean up. Once the mess was handled, he stood up and with his hands full of broken dishes, he announced to the entire dining room, "We're all about working together here at The Gilford House Inn. Thank you to everyone for joining us and please enjoy your meal. If you need anything, someone is always here to help."

Then he looked down at the young woman still picking up shards of dishes and said in a genuine tone, "Go ahead and take ten, Janette. I know it gets stressful sometimes, so catch your breath and come back in when you're ready."

She looked up at him with wide eyes full of surprise and thanked him profusely before walking outside where I saw her light up what was surely a much-needed cigarette. She glanced back through the window with a confused expression, as if to wonder if what had just happened had in fact happened, and I was just as surprised as she was.

I couldn't deny it. Zane's response to the accident impressed me. I wanted very much to believe in him and that he was truly making an effort to be a better boss to his staff. Still, there was that small part of me that wondered if he was doing it just to impress me. Had he seen me hiding in that alcove?

But was it so awful if he was actually trying to show me he could be a better person?

Yes, a person needed to want to change for themselves, but if I could inspire him to be better to his people, then wasn't it all worth it in the long run?

I rounded the corner as he made his way into another portion of the inn and caught the eye of the check-in clerk, Mandy. She smiled wide and flipped her very blonde hair over her shoulder as she set the book she'd been reading down on the desk in front of her.

"I think you might be having a good influence on him. We're all really very happy and thankful for that, by the way."

Shaking my head, I smiled. "I don't think I can take the credit for this."

"Pardon me for saying it ma'am, but I think you're wrong," she said as she looked around to make sure Zane couldn't hear her. "We've all noticed whenever you're here, he's much nicer to be around. More than one of the girls has commented that we wish we could move you in permanently. It's as though he's a whole different person when you're here."

A guest walked by and waved, mentioning something about taking a stroll in the garden, and Mandy wished her a good day before turning to look at me. "It's true. He's just nicer when you're around."

"I've never had that effect on anyone before, so I highly doubt that it's because of me. I think he must have some other reason for being so nice."

She shrugged, but the twinkle in her eye told me she didn't believe me. "Well, we'll see. What-ever the reason is, you have to admit he's not so bad when he ditches the whole angry ogre act. He's almost attractive. You know, in a Doctor Jekyll and Mr. Hyde way, I guess," she teased.

Mandy may have been young, but she'd

witnessed the same thing I had a few minutes earlier. As I walked outside, turning my collar up to avoid the chill, I had to admit that seeing that other side to Zane gave me a genuinely good feeling about him.

There was no way he could have seen me from where I was standing, which meant that his being kind to that young woman must have been him truly trying to make an effort.

The people who worked at the inn were all good people, and if my being around helped someone, then I was happy to be a good influence. Still, I wanted Zane to do it for himself, as well.

As my shoes crunched over the leaves, I made my way back to the bridge where we'd argued. Mandy hit the nail on the head when she mentioned that when he wasn't acting like an ogre, he wasn't so bad. In fact, he could be quite charming when he wanted to be.

I ran my hand on the red wood rails and let out a content sigh as I looked out into the woods around me. Whatever happened, I was going to do a great job promoting my favorite getaway place.

✧   ✧   ✧

COZY IN MY room sipping some hot cocoa I had

brought up from the dining room, I heard voices coming from the hallway outside my door. I recognized the male voice as Zane's and walked over to the door and listened, quickly realizing the female's voice belonged to the maid I had seen him berate there months ago. She said something in a meek voice I couldn't understand, but it was Zane I heard clearly first.

"I'm sorry for yelling at you like that… ummm…"

I heard a long pause before he continued. "I'm so sorry, but I don't even know your name. I yelled at you and I didn't even bother to find out your name."

Quietly, the maid said, "It's Lucy, sir."

"Lucy, I'm sorry for being so disrespectful that day I yelled at you in front of a guest. I shouldn't have acted that way in front of any of the guests here, and I shouldn't have acted that way period. You deserve more respect than that."

I pushed my ear to the door since the maid spoke so painfully quiet and abandoned my hot cocoa all together. Maybe Zane had changed.

"Thank you, Mr. Gilford. I appreciate that."

"No, I don't deserve thanks for an apology that's so late. I just needed you to now that I'm sorry, and I'd like to put it in the past, if that's okay with you, Lucy."

I heard the smile in Lucy's voice as she said,

"Okay. Thank you so much. I really do love working here at the inn. Your mother was a great lady and an even more wonderful boss. We all miss her and want to see you as happy here as she was."

At that point, I strained against the door to hear Zane since his voice had dropped considerably, but I did hear him say, "Thank you. That would be nice. Have a good night, Lucy."

Even though nothing they said had anything to do with me, I couldn't help feel happy for Lucy and for Zane too. Still leaning against the door, I heard footsteps muted on the soft carpet coming towards my room, and then they stopped. Anticipation hung heavy in the air for a long moment as I stood behind my door holding my breath, knowing Zane stood just on the other side.

Then came a knock on the door. I knew I shouldn't let him in because I still wanted to keep things strictly professional between us. I hadn't forgotten the past we shared, and even as I felt happy to see him being a better man to his employees, I wondered if he could ever truly change.

As all these thoughts raced through my mind, my arm extended and my hand grabbed the doorknob, turning it. I opened the door to see him standing there, and that cockiness that so often colored his expression and body language was missing. Instead, the man who stood facing me looked different.

Like I was the only person in the world who mattered to him at that moment.

"Zane..."

"Becca, I hoped you were still awake. Can I come in?"

A tug of war between my head and my body quickly ended with my desire for him winning, and I stepped back to let him into my room. "Sure."

Sure was the last thing I felt, but I ignored the warnings my brain was sending out and closed the door. He turned around to look at me, and I saw in his eyes he wanted me as much as I wanted him.

"You know, when I first saw you that day in the hallway, I couldn't believe my eyes. It seemed unbelievable that you, of all people, would be standing right there in front of me again," he said, slowly inching his way toward me.

Some part of me wanted to move away from him, but I remained where I stood because I didn't want to let that part control me anymore. What happened in the past couldn't be changed, but maybe we were different people now. I knew I certainly had changed and what I'd just heard in the hall told me Zane had too.

Maybe things could be different now.

"You look even more beautiful than you did back in California, Becca. You haven't changed much at all."

He stopped right in front of me, so close that it was almost too close. I tilted my head up and looked into his dark eyes staring down at me with that look of desire in them I remembered all too well.

"I have changed, Zane. I've changed a lot."

My gaze slid down his gorgeous body, and I had to admit that hadn't changed. Still as muscular and seductive as ever, Zane still looked like the Greek god he'd looked like when I first met him.

He reached out to caress my cheek, and my skin heated at his touch. This was the effect he always had on me, and for the first time since we ended all those years ago, I wanted to let myself go with him.

Leaning in, he whispered against my lips, "The part of you I could never get enough of is still the same. That's never going to change."

His mouth met mine, and instantly, God, everything about him began to overwhelm me. The scent of his skin, so masculine and earthy. The taste of the whisky he'd drank at dinner. The feel of his lips crushing mine with the need to possess me like he always had.

If any part of me wanted to pull away at that moment, it remained silent as I surrendered to the man who I'd never fully put in my past. Hurriedly, I unbuttoned his shirt and slid it off his broad shoulders to see even here in Vermont, his skin was tan and his body could still turn heads on the beach.

I leaned back and ran my hands down over his chest to his washboard abs, my fingertips tracing the peaks and valleys of his muscles to where his pants sat low on his hips. Zane watched where my hands travelled and moaned when I dragged my forefinger from one hip to another.

He made quick work of his pants and threw them off to the side before turning his attention back to me. His hands seemed to move at lightning speed, removing my clothes in a flash as I tried to catch my breath. Zane was the same incredible and seductive force he'd always been.

In that way, nothing had changed.

Easing me back on the bed, he laid me down and kissed me hard, making my head spin with anticipation. I wanted to feel him inside me, filling me up completely again. I slid my hands down his back and sunk my fingernails into his skin to urge him on.

"Please…don't make me wait, Zane," I moaned.

He lifted his head and smiled wickedly. "I

love when you beg. It gets me so hard."

I wrapped my legs around his waist and dug my heels into his lower back. "Fuck me…God, you're such a tease."

Reaching down between us, he gripped his cock and gave me what I wanted, sliding it into me slowly. I arched my back to take all of him, loving the feeling of being completely filled.

"Christ, Becca, you're still so fucking tight. You feel so good," he moaned as he began to piston in and out of my needy pussy.

My entire body hummed with pleasure with each time his cock touched that spot deep inside me. I clutched his shoulders and his hips pushed forward and then pulled back, thrilling me and inching me toward my orgasm.

Zane kissed me long and deep, taking me to a place that made my eyes roll back into my head. My thighs began to quiver against his sides, signaling the beginning of that sublime feeling that came from release.

"I'm…oh, God…don't stop!" I cried, raking my fingernails down his spine as he pumped hard into me, sending my body into overdrive.

I slipped into ecstasy while Zane thrust into me one last time before collapsing onto me and groaning low and deep in my ear. The sound of pure masculinity filled my head, taking me to another level of pleasure only he had ever given me.

The two of us lay there in silence for a long time, reveling in the exquisite feelings we'd created in one another again. Just as every other time with him, the sex was mind blowing. No other man had been able to take my body to the heights Zane could.

But would that be enough?

CHAPTER FOURTEEN

Zane

M Y EYES OPENED, and before my brain even registered what time of day it was, I knew I was right where I should be. Becca lay beside me still asleep, her long brown hair hiding part of her beautiful face as she snored quietly. I watched her, amazed at how sweet she looked there all curled up on my shoulder. Ordinarily, I wouldn't have thought that snoring could be cute, but somehow, she made it almost adorable.

I slid my arm to wrap it around her, trying not to wake her, but her eyes fluttered open and she looked at me. Smiling, I tucked her hair behind her ear so I could see her entire face.

"Good morning. I'm sorry I woke you. I didn't mean to. I was just watching you sleep. And snore. You're really cute when you snore, you know that?"

Her dark eyebrows drew in, and she frowned. "Morning," she said groggily.

Not exactly the kind of reception I'd hoped for or expected, but maybe she wasn't a morning person. Hell, before I came back here, I wasn't a morning person either, but being awakened every day by one calamity or another had made me one in the past few months.

I draped my arm over her and began to rub my face into the nape of her neck, but she shied away immediately. Confused, I wondered if my snoring comment had bothered her. Based on the noises she'd been making all night and the way her body had reacted, I thought there would be some kind of happiness from her in the morning.

Or at least a little sweetness.

Instead, she acted downright chilly as she shrugged me off and hurried into the bathroom, emerging fully clothed in less than a minute. Basically shooing me away, she said, "I have to leave to go back to the city, but I'll be back up this weekend to talk about what I have planned for the advertising campaign."

I sat up in bed, stunned by her words. Had I done something wrong? The last I recalled, we'd spent a fantastic night fucking one another's brains out, and now she was acting like I was some high school boyfriend and her parents were coming through the door at any second.

"Sure, Becca. No problem," I said as I nodded in amazement that we wouldn't be having another round this morning and watched her buzz around the room, packing up like the place was on fire.

I stood from the bed and stretched before I gathered up my clothes from the previous night. I didn't exactly rush as I dressed, in no hurry for our first night together to end so abruptly. I stepped into my pants, and out of the corner of my eye, I saw Becca glaring at me as if I was keeping her from something more important.

"So you have to head back even before breakfast?" I asked while I slipped my shirt over my shoulders.

She barely answered, giving me a curt "Uh huh" as she watched me slowly button up my shirt.

In all honesty, I had no idea what the problem could be, but I sure as hell didn't want to ask her what was wrong. I could have gladly spent another hour or two in bed with her.

The old me would have pressed her for more sex, completely ignoring her desire to leave so soon, but I was really trying to be a nicer guy for her, and I figured nice guys didn't press an obviously hurried woman back into bed. It would have been easy to take her in my arms and pull her to me, kissing her neck in that way that drove her wild, but she wanted to go, and it seemed wrong to try and manipulate her into staying, even if I did want to bury my cock in her some more.

This whole nice guy thing didn't feel so fucking fabulous when I had to watch the woman I'd just slept with inching toward the door like I had the plague or something. She grabbed her bag and purse along with her briefcase, juggling the three of them and nearly falling over in the process, so I extended my hand and took her suitcase for her.

She looked up at me with a mixture of anger and confusion on her face I couldn't understand. "Zane, you don't have to do that."

"Becca, I don't mind. It's not a big deal. Let me help you."

"I really don't need you to. I don't need any more special treatment. The staff has already gone out of their way for me, and I don't need to be treated like some delicate flower who can't carry her own bags, okay? I'm fine all on my own."

She tried to wrestle the suitcase from my grip and nearly toppled over. Catching her, I steadied her on her feet and said, "Stop. Becca, please. This is a hotel. Someone is bound to grab a bag for you, so it might as well be the man you just slept with. Don't worry. Let's just get you downstairs and checked out, okay?"

She stared up at me with that look of confusion in her eyes I still didn't understand and forced a smile. Why she had to force a smile at all baffled me, though. As we silently walked down to the lobby, neither of us saying a word, I ran through the evening we'd just spent together and wondered what had gone wrong.

We'd had an incredible time together, hadn't we? I'd thought we did while she was moaning my name and begging me not to stop.

Great sex. Check. Hell, it had been mind-blowing. Hadn't it?

Sweet afterglow time together lying in each other's arms like women loved? Check. We'd even had a few laughs as we came down from that great sex high.

So what the hell had happened between when we drifted off to sleep and when we woke up a few minutes ago?

Right before we reached the check-in desk, I said quietly, "You'll be up again next weekend?"

Becca nodded but didn't look at me when she answered, "Yeah. I'll be back here on Saturday morning."

She checked out with Mandy and we walked out with her bags to her car, still saying nothing. I loaded them in her trunk, becoming more than a little put off by how cold she was acting. Sure, we'd had a rocky to start, but I really thought we'd broken through some kind of barrier in Becca's mind when we got together last night.

Apparently, I had been wrong.

Without even a kiss, she gave me a simple goodbye and got into her car. Before I knew it, I stood there watching her driving away. Confused about what had happened, I shrugged and slowly made my way toward the front porch of the inn when my phone began to ring. Looking down at the screen, I saw it was Stacey, my ex from California.

I rolled my eyes and sighed. What could she possibly want? I hadn't left anything of mine with her and had nothing of hers, so it wasn't like we had anything to settle. I hesitated before pressing the answer button but did anyway.

"What is it, Stacey?"

"Zane, honey, I'm so glad you answered. I know we haven't talked in like, forever, but listen, I'm in town for my sister's wedding in Boston, and I want to see you. I know we didn't exactly leave on the best of terms, but maybe you could make an exception for me? Pretty pretty please?" she cooed, the flirtiness in her voice a clear sign she was laying it on thick.

I hated when she called me honey. It never failed to grate on my nerves, and she should have remembered that. I cringed as soon as I heard her say it in that annoying cutesy girl voice. It didn't make me want to listen to another thing she said, much less see her. How had I not realized for so long how annoying that affected tone of hers was?

"Stacey, I'm pretty busy," I said flatly, not in the mood for another woman leading me on.

"Too busy for me? I can't believe that."

Then I realized how good it would feel to show her I had moved on and had found someone a thousand times the woman she was in the brains department alone. It had hurt more than I wanted to admit when I found out she'd moved on from me within a month of my leaving California. It was a shit move, and I wanted her to know I hadn't been held back because of it.

More importantly, I wanted her to know that I was better off without her.

"I don't know, Stacey. I've kind of got my hands full with work up here."

"But Zane, don't you want to see your favorite girl? I know you miss me," she said in that sugary sweet voice she always put on during sex.

"What do we even have to talk about, Stacey? I feel like we left things on a pretty final note."

"Oh, come on. Please? For me? Think of all the stuff we have to catch up on. I've been trying this new workout routine, and I know you want to see the results," she purred into the phone.

Stacey only had one move. Sex. Typical for someone who only had her looks to carry her since she lacked the brains and intellect to attract someone. So she used her body to get what she wanted. It had worked for her pretty well her whole adult life.

And it had worked like a charm on me.

"I guess. I don't know how much free time I'll have for you. Things are pretty busy here at the inn."

"Oh, stop it. You and I both know you don't care if shit is busy in that dump. You'll make time for me. I know you. Just hand off all of that managerial crap to some assistant or whatever they have up there in the sticks. It'll be great. A nice little getaway reunion for the two of us. We can even spend most of our time away from that place since I bet it smells like old people and sadness. Is there even Wi-Fi there?"

"Yeah, Stacey, of course, there's...ugh, nevermind. Fine. You know where I am."

I ended the call not happy that I'd see my ex but at least pleased that she'd see when I had no interest in getting back together with her that I'd moved on. But the next day I woke up to my phone vibrating with a text message. I hoped it was from Becca, but a glance at my phone told me it was Stacey.

Hey, Zane! I won't be able to make it up to you until the weekend. Sorry! I'll see you then!

I let out a sigh and ran my hands through my

hair as I tossed the phone away from me. I really didn't want Stacey around while Becca was there. I considered texting her just not to come since the last thing I wanted was her crashing what I was trying to do.

But I knew her too well. She'd just show up on her own and ruin everything. Better to control the situation myself and keep the two women far away from one another.

THE NEXT FEW days dragged by as I waited for the weekend, but I focused on being kind to the staff and mainly keeping to myself. I worried about Becca and Stacey being at the inn at the same time and how to perfectly manage it and didn't want to take it out on everyone else, so better to hide away as much as possible to avoid biting someone's head off. By the time the weekend came, I was a bundle of nerves and more than ready to get out of my office.

Stacey arrived first and didn't see me on the stairs, but I saw her when she walked in. As tan as ever with platinum blonde hair that fell to nearly the small of her back, she certainly turned heads in a fire engine red dress that hugged her body like a second skin and barely reached the middle of her thighs.

In all honesty, she stuck out like a sore thumb against the quaint backdrop of the inn. She didn't look any different than I remembered her, but there was something about her that didn't seem as attractive as it always had to me. I didn't feel that intense need to have her naked under me, and as I heard her voice, she sounded slightly annoying. As she addressed Mandy at the check-in desk, I realized for the first time what an utter bitch she could be.

"Listen, whoever you are, I know the owner, Zane," she said when Mandy politely explained to her that we didn't have any rooms available for her.

"Yes, of course Mrs…" Mandy said in her sweet voice.

In fact, the business had been doing well, and we were at full capacity. Nothing Mandy said to her was wrong, and she'd told her the truth in her usual professional way.

"Just find him. I'm sure he can clear up your stupid mistake."

"Yes, Mrs…"

"It's miss, thank you very much. I'm not some old hag like the rest of the people here. Seriously, is this a hotel or a retirement home?"

"Sorry, miss," Mandy said, looking wounded by her swipe at the inn.

Feelings of protectiveness rose up in me at Stacey's rudeness, and I walked over to get her away as quickly as possible. "Mandy, I can handle this."

"Hello, Mr. Gilford. This woman says she knows you, but I'm sorry to inform you that there are no rooms available. Everything is booked until Monday, including Becca's room. I really don't have a way to move anything around without canceling someone else's reservation."

Before I could get a word in, Stacey interjected, "Then I'll just be staying wherever Zane stays, right, honey?"

I didn't feel like getting into a discussion about it in front of my employee, so I quickly ushered her away from the lobby as she muttered, "Jeez, that one is kind of an idiot, isn't she?"

Rolling my eyes, I worked to contain my irritation and suddenly wished that I hadn't agreed to have her come at all.

"Can you help me with some of this? Jesus!" she whined from behind me as we started up the stairs.

I grabbed two of the four bags she had with her and began lugging them up to the second floor. Christ, it felt like I was carrying suitcases full of bricks, which told me I'd probably grabbed the two that were full of shoes she wouldn't even use that weekend. Only a goddamned centipede would need that many pairs of shoes.

The door to my room barely closed behind us before I turned around and saw her standing naked in front of me with a fuck me expression on her face.

"I missed you so much, Zane. As soon as I knew my sister's wedding would be nearby, I knew I had to see you again."

She lay down on the bed and beckoned me closer. I sat down, not interested in doing anything with her. Gently pushing her away, I said, "So what happened with that guy you were with? Does he know you're naked here on my bed offering me sex?"

Stacey ran her hands down the front of my pants and palmed my cock through the fabric. "Don't be like that. You know how it is with us. We can't deny what our bodies want. You know that."

What I knew was she wasn't the woman I wanted anymore.

I stood from the bed and tossed her dress on the bed next to her. "I have to get back down to the lobby. This place can't seem to go ten minutes without some problem or another popping up. Stay here and don't leave. I'll bring us up some food, and we'll have a bite to eat."

Her mouth dropped open in shock, but I didn't wait around to hear a response. Just like when she moved on after I left California, I didn't care enough to bother.

A few minutes later, Stacey showed up in the

dining room and sat down at table with me. My heart began to slam into my chest in terror that at any minute Becca might walk in and see us together.

Stacey immediately began to prattle on about some new makeup line she'd found while I'd been away. Something about it being vegan or some inane shit like that, like always. It was never a real conversation with Stacey, never anything of substance. Just crap. She would go on and on about the shallowest nonsense anyone had ever heard, and I would zone out and think of the football game from the night before or anything else until she eventually stopped.

I hardly listened to her as my brain whirled at the situation that might blow up in my face at any time. Just then, I looked up and saw Becca being shown to her seat at her usual table across the room. The look on her face told me she was more than a little surprised to see me sitting there with another woman.

Fuck.

I saw Becca trying to be sly about spying on us, but she wasn't the type to hide her emotions very well, and I could read her like a book. She kept looking over at the two of us, and I knew what she saw bothered her.

Fuck. Everything I had worried about all week was slowly happening before my eyes.

Looking across the table, I interrupted Stacey in the middle of whatever she was saying. "We need to go upstairs."

She shook her head and wrinkled her nose. "What? Zane, are you even listening to me right now?"

"Yeah, sure, let's go."

"What was the last thing I said?"

"Something about makeup or whatever. Come on. We need to go upstairs. I have something I want to show you."

She nodded with a sly grin, thinking I wanted her when all I wanted was to get the hell out of there. We stood up, and I could practically feel the jealousy wafting across the room from Becca as we walked over.

This wasn't going well.

I had to say something to her. I couldn't just walk out of the dining room with Stacey hanging all over me without saying hello to Becca. We walked up to her table, and I saw just how bad things were already. She pretended she didn't see us coming toward her, but I knew her well enough to know that she never missed a thing.

Worst of all, her expression said she wasn't just angry. She was hurt.

CHAPTER FIFTEEN

Becca

LEGS. THAT'S ALL I saw. Legs that went on forever. Legs that made me look down at my own as I sat at my usual table in the dining room and cringe at how incredibly average length my legs were.

I'd always thought my legs were my best part of my body, but one look at the legs on the blonde with Zane made me doubt what I'd believed since I was a teenage girl. So much for decades of confidence.

How strange that a single person could make an accomplished woman with a fair amount of self-confidence feel so much less simply because she existed. Other women didn't typically intimidate me, but I couldn't deny it. Sitting there looking at Zane with the tall blonde with those legs and a body that surely had to have been bought and paid for bothered me.

There was no way breasts sat that high and

large naturally. They defied gravity and basic physics altogether.

I thought a few more nasty thoughts about her, mostly focused on the fact that she didn't even look like a real human being and more like some tacky Barbie come to life, before silently scolding myself for acting like the kinds of women I disliked and looking back down at my menu. I wasn't a catty woman or the type to put another woman down just to make myself feel better. It simply wasn't my way, and I didn't approve of women who tore one another down like that.

After all, Zane wasn't mine. I had made it abundantly clear that he wasn't every single time he had tried to be. Well, every single time but that last one. Against my better judgment, I'd slept with him, and the very next time he knew I'd be here, he trotted out her?

How dare he treat me like some school girl whose emotions had no meaning to him? It was crass, and I had no time for crass. I wanted to kick myself for having slept with him the weekend before. I had known it was a dumb move then, and he proved it to me every minute he sat there with that life-size Barbie.

As the waiter asked me for my order, I gave it to him hastily and could have sworn I saw pity in his eyes. I looked around, and it felt like the entire room, especially the staff, was looking at me.

What a sucker they must see me as!

At a place like the inn, gossip traveled fast, and they probably knew Zane and I had something going on. I shook my head to dispel the thought. No, we hadn't.

Zane and the blonde stood to leave, and I looked over, trying to glean how serious they were from body language alone. When had all this with the new woman happened since I had thought he'd been chasing me?

What a fool I'd been! Had I just been something to pass the time while he waited for this woman to show up?

Before I could get too deeply into those thoughts, Zane and the woman approached my table, forcing me to deal with them.

"Hey there, Becca."

I gave him a small smile and a nod, not wanting to betray how I felt, even as I wanted to smack his face.

"This is Stacey, an old friend of mine," he explained with a smug smile. How had I ever even thought that smile was charming?

His old friend Stacey giggled and playfully slapped Zane on the shoulder as she purred, "Old friend, my ass. We were together for two years, and in all that time I don't recall us ever doing anything friends do together. Maybe friends with benefits, but not friends."

I looked up at him as I tried to mask the emotions that began to bubble up inside me. Anger, jealousy, and hurt all blended into a Molotov cocktail of feelings that threatened to explode from me if I didn't keep them in check. I pushed them down and focused on keeping my cool. Zane Gilford had just proved to me that he wasn't worth me getting all emotional over, least of all in public, and I wasn't going to give him the satisfaction of letting him know I was upset.

Zane cringed and laughed nervously. "We've known each other for a long time. She lives in California, so when I came East, we broke up."

I didn't say anything and did my best to keep my face emotionless as Stacey responded by squeezing him tightly to those fake breasts of hers and kissing him hard on the cheek before saying with a huge grin, "But now that I'm on this coast for a while, that whole breaking up thing won't be lasting very long. Right, Zane?"

He didn't say anything, so she looked at me and smirked. "We just can't stay apart. Besides, why would we want too, right?"

I held in the murderous rage that coiled inside me as I looked at him and said, "Well, when you have time, Zane, I'd like to discuss the campaign. I'll be here until tomorrow afternoon, but then I have to head back to the city for an important meeting."

Zane nodded, but as he opened his mouth to answer, the annoying blonde interjected, "Well, I'm not sure he'll be able to make that appointment. Sorry, sweetie. We have a lot of lost time to make up for. That might be something you need to reschedule with his staff. Granted, they aren't very competent, so try and speak slowly for them."

My hands curled at my sides. I hated hearing her insult the staff I knew to be good people who tried hard to run the inn and keep it like it had been under Zane's mother.

Quickly, Zane said, "I look forward to hearing your ideas, Becca. I'll let you know what time I'm free tomorrow morning."

Without another word, he hurried the two of them away. I got a quick glance over the shoulder from Barbie on his arm that told me exactly what the two of them were off to do. Clearly, they were both in a hurry to get upstairs and get out of their clothes.

I shouldn't have been so damned foolish to believe that Zane Gilford could be anything but the kind of guy who flaunts a woman like that in front of the one he'd spent the night with just a week before. I sat staring at the food on my plate, but I had no interest in eating anymore.

Why did any of this bother me anyway? I didn't want to be with him, so I shouldn't have been so hurt by his behavior. Still, I shouldn't have slept with him. I knew that the next morning. But I couldn't help but be filled with immense regret over that.

He was an ass, and I had always known that.

If only I'd listened to my gut.

I looked out the window and saw rain begin to pour down, mirroring how I felt. I couldn't take it one more second. I decided to abandon my food and the dining room altogether since sitting there made me feel exposed and humiliated. As I hurried past the check-in desk towards the stairs, Mandy gave me a look of pity that only made things worse.

And then, as I walked up the stairs to hide away in my room for the rest of the day, my phone vibrated and my day instantly became ten times worse.

"What do you want, Dustin?" I asked sharply, not bothering to hide the anger in my voice.

If there was one person who I didn't care to manage my tone around, it was my annoying ex. Sure, he might have been getting some overflow from the anger I felt towards Zane, but I simply didn't care.

Dustin or Zane. The difference between them at that moment didn't seem much.

"You should watch that tone of yours, Becca. It's what got you into this mess in the first place."

Dustin smugly said, angering me further with his cocky attitude.

"This mess? Are you implying we divorced because of my bad attitude? I'm sorry, Dustin. Maybe my memory isn't serving me, but I think your proclivity for sleeping with other women probably hurt us more than my bad attitude."

"There you go again. Do you ever take responsibility for anything? Maybe there was a reason I didn't want you and wanted someone else."

Disgusted already with how this conversation had turned, I began to take the stairs two at a time. "Well, you sure picked a winner, Dustin. How's that gold digging bitch of yours doing? Still going into debt with your lawyer trying to get a townhouse to sell to fund the lavish lifestyle you can't afford?"

My words were hateful and rude, and I meant every syllable from the bottom of my heart. I was sick of the men in my life thinking they could just walk all over me. The time had come to let this one have it.

"Sure, Becca, keep digging your grave. You know, you'll never find love if you're such a bitch all the time. It's not like you have any other redeeming qualities except your bank account to fall back on."

"Why are you calling me? We agreed to keep

things between our lawyers. Your voice isn't on my list of things I'm interested in hearing, so whatever you have to say, you need to say it or get the fuck off this phone call before I hang up on you."

"Wow, real nice Becca."

"Fuck you, Dustin."

"Nice. Well, I wanted you to know your lawyer will hear from my new one. Her name is Angela Wolfson. Maybe you've heard of her?"

I stopped on the landing between the second and third floors and took a deep breath in. That explained the arrogance in his voice. I had heard of her. Other authors called her a powerhouse. She was widely regarded as the nastiest and most effective divorce lawyer in Manhattan, and she had a track record of winning every case that came her way. Some said it was because of her pit bull-like-viciousness. Others claimed she had an almost mob-like connection within the system. Whatever it was, she was a force to be reckoned with.

I stood there in the hallway leaning against the wall stunned, mostly at how Dustin would have been able to afford such a formidable lawyer. My head began to spin. Could this day get any worse?

"I'm going to guess by your silence you have heard of her. Good. I'm getting that townhouse, Becca. Make sure you keep it clean for the people I end up selling it to. I don't want to have to pay for some cleaning crew to get that stink of lavender you love so much out of every square inch. I'd keep that attitude in check too. The judge isn't going to like what a bitch you are, and at this rate, you'll be losing that townhouse sooner than you think. My gold digging bitch and I will love selling it right out from underneath you."

With that he hung up, leaving me there with the phone to my ear and the overwhelming need to cry like a baby. I rushed to my room on auto-pilot. I didn't want to be around anyone, including the staff that passed me on the stairs and in the hallway who kept giving me looks that told me my emotions were written all over my face.

I shut the door behind me, and before I knew it, the tears began streaming down my face. I closed my eyes and collapsed on the bed, letting my head hit the pillow and hoping I could forget about how bad my day had suddenly become. Much like the weather outside raging against the glass window panes in my room, when it rained it poured, and it sure was raining a lot in my life now.

Dustin didn't have to be such an ass, yet he never failed to be just that, but he wasn't a big surprise. Zane, however, had been. I couldn't get the thought of that woman hanging all over him out of my mind, and I had the horrible feeling that somewhere in that hotel while I cried into my pillow, Zane was fucking her into his.

The thought only made the whole situation worse. I couldn't help it, though, and I decided just to let myself have a good long cry. Why couldn't I attract good men who didn't want to take my home from me or throw women like that life-sized Barbie in my face after having sex with me?

What did it matter? There was nothing else to be done about Zane or what we'd done together, and for once, I didn't want to be the problem solver or the strong one. I simply wanted to cry.

CHAPTER SIXTEEN

Zane

S TACEY RECLINED ON my bed, ready for what she thought we came back to my room to do, and grinned as she put her hands behind her head. "Someone was in a hurry for us to be alone."

I turned my back on her and sat down at my desk to check out some paperwork on the inn's business insurance that I'd been neglecting. I had zero interest in talking to her. If I was honest, I didn't want to waste any more of my time dealing with her further as she'd seriously been getting on my nerves from the minute she arrived.

When I didn't respond to her come hither thing she had going on, she came up behind me and wrapped her arms around my shoulders. I didn't react, so she blew softly in my ear and whispered, "The bed's over there, baby."

Even her breathing irritated me, and I shrugged her off, not even wanting her to touch me. I had wanted to spend the weekend with Becca, but the look on her face when Stacey spoke to her made my stomach turn. Even worse, I didn't know if she would ever speak to me again other than about an advertising campaign I really didn't give a damn about.

Everything that could go wrong had gone wrong. Fucking terrific.

Stacey planted kisses along the side of my neck, and I gently pushed her away again. "Can you not, please? I'm busy, and I don't have time for whatever you're doing right now."

"Baby, come on. Isn't this why you told me we should come upstairs? You can finish that later. I'm here now. That's better than some stupid work for this shit hole, isn't it?" she said, leaning around me to give me that baby doll look she liked to use on men.

In the past, it would have been easy to shove my work aside and throw her down on the bed to fuck her brains out. Now, though, she repulsed me somehow. I didn't exactly know why, but the woman I'd been so unhappy about losing just a few weeks ago now meant nothing.

I rolled my eyes and went back to work, but she persisted. Finally, I snapped and said, "I don't want anything to do with you right now, Stacey. Scratch that. I just don't want anything to do with you. Period. Come to think of it, why the fuck are you even here again?"

She stood up and glared at me, twisting her phony face into an ugly grimace. "What the fuck is your problem? You're an asshole, you know that?"

The bitchy attitude of hers that I knew lurked below that plastic surface came roaring back. She flipped her long, straight hair over her shoulder and shot her right hip out, a signal that a big fight was just seconds from starting.

"Are you serious? How long did it take you to find someone new after I left California? Ten minutes? Fifteen? Why the fuck should I want anything to do with you?" I said, pushing myself back from my desk and finally seeing her for the childish little girl she truly was.

She put her hands on her hips and narrowed her eyes to angry slits. With a growl in her voice, she said, "We had all but broken up, and you know it, Zane. Besides, you're the one who ran away to this dump without even a second thought. Blah, blah, blah, my mom's will. You could have just stayed. Why don't you want me now? You seemed to be all ready to go downstairs."

For a moment, I stood there just looking at her and wondered how I could have spent so long with her. Did we have anything in common other than what we did in bed? Had we ever had a real conversation that didn't end in us fucking?

"There's someone else, okay? Is that what you need to hear? Just like you, I was able to move on too, so why don't you get over it and yourself in the process, okay?"

Her mouth dropped open and she looked stunned for a moment before backing away from me. "Are you serious? Who the hell is it? Is it someone I know? Is it someone from back home?"

I rolled my eyes and walked past her into the bathroom, splashing cold water on my face while I tried to calm myself down and avoid the fight that had already begun. I didn't want to discuss this with Stacey. I should have never agreed to see her. I looked in the mirror and saw the full truth of my mistake staring back at me in Stacey's angry eyes.

"You don't get to just walk away from me like that, you dick. Who is it? You need to start talking, now!"

"I don't feel like doing this right now, Stacey. I've had a long couple of months," I said as I tilted my head back and forth desperately trying to crack my neck to ease the stress from how this day had gone to hell.

"Fuck you! I don't give a rat's ass how long a couple of months you've had. Who is it?" she demanded.

Staring back at her as she stood behind me, I

thought about lying to her since I couldn't truly say Becca and I were together after what had happened downstairs, but then I said fuck it. She wanted to know who I'd moved on with? Good. I'd tell her.

"The woman downstairs. Her name is Becca. It's her, okay? Is that what you need to fucking hear? It's the beautiful woman downstairs with qualities and intelligence you'll never have. Is that what I need to say to you to get you to leave me the fuck alone?" I shouted at her, my hands gripping the edge of the sink as I stared back at her in the mirror.

Her expression looked like someone had slapped her across the face. Hurt slowly filled her eyes, surprising me, but then it morphed into anger that began to roll off her in waves. As if she didn't know what to say, she stood there just staring at me until she finally broke the silence.

"Why aren't you together then?"

That question didn't have a good answer. At least it didn't have an answer that made me feel good about anything I'd done.

Stacey took a step back into my room and shook her head. "I know what you're doing. Oh, my God! I know! You didn't tell me you were with someone because you wanted to use me to make her jealous. That's it, isn't it?"

I didn't say a word. Part of me wondered if

she was right. Had I subconsciously wanted that?

"Do you realize what a dick you are, Zane? I might have fucked up by seeing other people when you left, but you're a real piece of work for doing that to some new girl. What is wrong with you? Are you even capable of having a real emotion without fucking it up for yourself? I wasn't always perfect. I get that, but for fuck's sake, what is wrong with you?"

I sighed and turned around, feeling defeated. She wasn't totally wrong. We had all but broken up when I had told her I wouldn't be returning to California. Sure, we had mentioned we would see one another again, but we both knew what was happening when I left her back there.

"Stacey…"

"No. You know what, Zane? Just…just fucking don't. You were right about one thing. I should have never come here," she said as she walked back into the room and grabbed her things.

Following her, I said, "Let me get the bags."

She spun around and barked, "Just stay away from me. I'll have one of your people take them for me."

I heard her order someone in the hallway to get her suitcases, and in a second, a young guy I'd only met once stood at my door looking unsure which one of us he wanted to deal with.

"That woman told me to get her bags, Mr. Gilford," he explained in a shaky voice.

I waved him into my room and handed him two of Stacey's suitcases. "I'll get the other two and follow you downstairs."

He quickly lifted the bags and hurried after her. Still a little stunned at all that had happened in the past hour, I picked up the other two and slowly headed down to the lobby to find her walking out the front door.

By the time I reached her car, she was already sitting inside. I put the suitcases in the trunk and closed it. Before I could reach her, she floored the gas and tore out of the parking lot, leaving me for the second time in a week watching a woman driving at top speed to get away from me.

I should have felt more sadness over it, but that would have been a lie. I never had any true feeling for her, as horrible as that sounded. We used each other and now that had ended. I'd gotten exactly what I deserved. It just hadn't turned out to be what I had wanted.

A few people on the front porch looked away as I walked back inside the inn. I saw Mandy at the check-in desk, and she quickly lowered her gaze and pretended to be busy doing work.

"Is Becca in her usual room?"

I couldn't tell if I was imagining it or not, but when Mandy looked up, her expression seemed to show disgust as she shook her head. "No, sir. She checked out about an hour ago. She did leave the work she did for the ad campaign with me, though."

Her words sounded professional, like always, but something in her eyes told me that she knew what had happened and didn't approve. It seemed everyone hated me at that moment. Who could blame them for believing I was an asshole like Stacey had said. A real dick. I should have just left well enough alone and kept on trying to be a good guy instead of trying to manipulate Stacey's visit.

I should have known what would happen.

I took the envelope that Mandy held out to me and walked away, disgusted with myself. I reached my room and closed the door behind me, wishing I could forget everything that happened.

Lying on my bed, I read through the proposals Becca created for the ad campaign for the inn. As I knew they would be, they were great. She captured the feel of the place I had to admit I'd never truly felt.

But she had. There in the plans her love for The Gilford House Inn came through loud and clear. She cared for the place like my mother had.

Like she always wished I would. But I never felt that about this inn.

Now I felt like garbage. I had only gone through her advertising agency to get closer to her. I didn't truly care about The Gilford House Inn doing any better. I only needed to keep it in the same successful shape that my mother had left it in. I'd never felt anything more than that.

It was always a means to an end.

And my ruse about advertising had all been to get Becca back to the inn. The thing was, it was so obvious that she cared about the inn that I felt like that much more of an asshole for doing what I had done to her.

I paced my room for a few minutes before grabbing my cell phone and dialing her number. My call went to voicemail, so in my best attempt to act casual and salvage the situation, I left a message.

"Hey, Becca! I just got the proposals for the advertising campaign, and I love them! The whole campaign looks incredible. Listen, give me a call back, okay? Talk to you soon."

Over the next two hours, I nearly wore out the carpet in my room as I paced back and forth waiting for her to return my call. I looked out the window over the grounds, walked into the bathroom and tried not to notice the shame written all over my face, and walked back out into the bedroom only to repeat the whole process over and over again.

Still, she didn't call.

Eventually, I broke down and picked up the

phone again, dialing her number as I wiped some of the sweat from my brow. Still, it went to voicemail, so I left a second message.

"Hey, Becca! It's Zane again. Just wanted to catch up with you about the campaign. As I mentioned before, it looks great! Please give me a call back when you get this."

But deep in my heart, I knew she wouldn't call back. Why would she? If I was lucky, she'd send me a vague and professional-sounding email or the even less personal mailed letter.

I lay back on my bed and stared at the room around me. For the first time at the inn, the overtly feminine room didn't bother me. I looked at the ideas Becca had for the campaign over and over again, and something about her love for The Gilford House Inn started to worm its way into me.

It wasn't that bad a place. It just wasn't my style. But somehow the flowery walls, the pinkish carpets, the doilies, and Thomas Kinkaid style paintings all came together and didn't look nearly as awful as I had always thought.

I grabbed my bottle of Jack and after a few drinks couldn't be in the room anymore, though. It had nothing to do with the style. I just felt trapped.

The whole Stacey thing had been stupid. There was nothing else to call it. I should have just told her to stay away, but instead I did what I always did and hurt a great woman who hadn't deserved it. Stacey's words echoed in my brain, and I couldn't stand it anymore.

I walked down to the dining room hoping to get some relief from my self-imposed torment of guilt and shame. The alcohol hadn't even made me feel better like it usually did. Instead, I just felt groggy and in desperate need of a cup of coffee.

Grabbing some from the break room, I sat down at my usual table by the window in the dining room. From there I could see the grounds, and the view made me think of when Becca was there. When I glanced up at the table next to me, I saw Mandy there drinking a cup of coffee too.

For the first time in my life, I asked her the question I imagined I could have asked any number of people who knew me over the years. "You don't like me very much, do you?"

She looked at me without much expression on her face before taking a deep breath and setting down her coffee down on the table to give me possibly the most honest answer I'd ever heard. "No, not really. I thought I did for a while there when you were so nice to everyone, but after today, that seems like it was all an act."

Her brutal honesty landed like a hard slap to my face. It was surprising to hear it from anyone, nevermind the young girl who checked people in at the front desk.

"I did ask. Well, I guess you know what this is all about for me then," I said, feeling defeated.

Had I been the only one who had thought for a moment that I could have been better? Was I that far gone?

Mandy took another sip from her coffee and said, "All I know is this, Mr. Gilford. Your mother was a wonderful woman who truly cared about people. She cared that they enjoyed their time here. She cared when one of her staff had a problem or when something good was happening in our lives outside of our jobs. She cared. I'm not sure what you care about, but it's nothing here. That's for sure."

I sat there wishing I could say she was wrong, but she wasn't. I looked around the dining room, letting the memories of when I was a child at the inn come back for a moment and smiled sadly as I looked back at Mandy.

"You know, when I was a little boy, maybe five or six, the idea of this all being mine was the best thing in the world. I'm not sure when that changed, but I didn't want this from my mother. I'm not the right kind of person for this place. This inn deserves someone who loves it and wants to see it shine. That's not me."

"You know who is?" she asked pointedly.

I knew before she answered her own question.

"Becca. She'd be perfect for this place."

She was right.

"You know what? You're right. She loves this place like my mother always wanted me to love it. Too bad she isn't the one who gets to have it."

The desk clerk nodded. "Yeah. Too bad. The place is always nicer when she's here too."

I knew what she meant and smiled as I stood to leave. "It is. It was nice talking to you, Mandy. Even if you don't like me very much."

She tipped her coffee to me and offered me what I thought was a small and sincere smile as I left to go back to my room.

CHAPTER SEVENTEEN

Becca

T HE DRIVE BACK home from Vermont seemed to take forever as I alternated between crying and shouting as I headed down the interstate. The other drivers must have thought I was insane as I screamed everything I wanted to say to Zane and a few things I wanted to say to that overly tanned, Barbie doll of a girlfriend of his. By the time I reached home, I'd lost my voice and I had no more tears left. I had only enough energy to climb into bed and pull the covers up over my head in my best attempt to forget everything that happened with Zane.

While I lay there as recriminations played on a loop in my head, I made a plan. Dive straight back into my work with a renewed vigor. It was the best kind of therapy and not only was it free, but it also put money back in my pocket.

Bright and early the next morning, my feet hit the pavement and I pressed my nose tightly to the grindstone. I got through three projects in record time, and my clients raved they were stunned that I had powered through with such great work so quickly. I smiled and accepted their compliments, but on the inside only I knew there was truly no other option for me.

For the second time, I had allowed Zane Gilford to hurt me, and I couldn't just sit around moping about it. I had to power through by whatever means possible.

One night, I sat in my living room staring out at the skyline of New York City and the memory of gazing at the Vermont sky, clear of artificial light and studded with bright stars, rushed back into my mind. Choking back the tears, I pushed away thoughts of The Gilford House Inn.

That's how it always was with me. Better to ignore the pain and just shove it down. Who had time for sitting around crying about things anyway? Still, I silently chastised myself for believing that Zane Gilford could have been anything other than what he always had been back when he left me high and dry all those years ago.

An unfeeling jerk and an asshole.

And I'd let myself get fooled by him for a second time.

Just like that, I found myself falling back into the memory of how it had all ended the first time with Zane. I'd done a great job of compartmental-izing those memories and hiding them in a box deep inside, but it seemed they wanted to come back anyway. Memories had a way of sneaking up on someone like that, and I was no more immune than anyone else.

The sun beat down on us while Zane and I walked along the sand, a pretty romantic time for two people who'd started out together with a quickie at a friend's party. I never thought I'd see him again after that night, but Zane Gilford had pursued me like a man on a mission. Texts, calls, flowers—he'd done all the right things to get me to fall for him.

And fall for him I did. Hard and fast. Before I knew it, I couldn't think of anything but him. He seemed just as into me too. We never said we loved one another, but we certainly acted like it.

That late August day, we headed up to Santa Monica Pier and ate way too much junk food as the sun set. Things had been going so well, and I thought we were getting ready to take another step forward by telling one another how we truly felt.

We didn't that night, but I had a feeling it was just a matter of time. Then one night he just didn't call. I called him and got his voicemail and figured he just fell asleep.

Three days later, my confusion morphed into

worry. What if he had gotten into an accident? How naïve I was then. Never the one to jump to the conclusion that someone would intentionally hurt me, I paced back and forth for hours in my room wondering if something terrible had happened to him.

A few days later, our mutual friend who had thrown the party we met at told me that he had moved to San Diego.

I returned to my senior year in college that fall brokenhearted. I never meant enough to him to get a decent goodbye. If we'd had some huge fight, maybe I could understand leaving without even a goodbye, but everything had seemed so perfect, even up until that last day we spent together.

Yet the next time I saw him all those years later, somehow he found a way to worm back into my heart. I had actually started to care for Zane Gilford again, despite what he'd done that summer. I hadn't admitted it to him or anyone but myself, but I honestly felt like something was growing between us. I wouldn't have slept with him if I hadn't been feeling something and if I hadn't sensed some genuine change in him. He seemed so much nicer to his staff and had even seemed to care more about the inn. I knew it wasn't a guarantee that he would fall madly in love with the place, but the effort I saw him exhibit had been enough to tell me he was on the road to change.

God, I had been so foolish! Everyone else saw him for exactly who he was, but I'd convinced myself he could change. So stupid.

Lifting my glass to my lips, I finished my drink and poured myself more wine. Tonight looked to be a full bottle night.

BURIED IN WORK, I sat at my desk and regretted the amount of wine I drank the night before, hating Zane even more and blaming my monster hangover on him. I heard a gentle knock on my door and looked up to see my assistant Amy peeking her head in.

"Hey, Becca. Do you have a minute?"

"Sure. Come on in. What's up?"

Amy took a seat in front of my desk, and I got up to sit in the one next to her after grabbing us each a diet soda. She may have been my assistant, but I hated talking to her from across my desk in such an official capacity all the time. My mother had always told me that when it came to business, not everything always had to be so businesslike.

She'd been with me since I started my agency four years ago and had grown to be more like a sister than just an assistant to me. It was often strange trying to make new friends as an adult in a huge city like New York, and I had been very grateful to meet Amy, someone I could go for drinks with and talk to even if we weren't at work. She had a healthy respect for me as her boss, but it was never awkward between us, especially when we were off the clock.

"Thanks, Becca. Listen, I wasn't going to say anything, but you've been moping around the office for days, and I can't just sit out there pretending like I can't tell," Amy said bluntly as she set the perspiring soda can down on a coaster on my desk.

"I don't know that I would say moping exactly. I mean, maybe a little off of my game, but moping?" I said, looking away as I took a sip of soda.

"Becca, your whole vibe is off, and you know I can read the vibes from a mile away. I know you like to bury yourself in work when things get tough, but you have to open up, girl. I keep asking why you're going out of town so often and you do the coy thing with me, and now you're back in town and sad. Things aren't adding up here, honey. I know Dustin is being his usual jackass self, but there's something else, isn't there? I don't want to push you to open up. Well, actually, yes I do, but only because I know it will be good for you. Come on, let it out. Dr. Amy is in the house."

Amy and her vibes. She never failed to cut to the heart of the issue at hand.

Chuckling at her bluntness, I nodded. "Okay, well, there's this guy I'd been seeing in Vermont."

It seemed like such a silly jumping off point, but isn't that how it had all began in the first place? I detailed for her the events of the past couple of months and explained the history between Zane and me. I didn't leave out any details, even the painful ones like how just a week after sleeping with me he paraded that blonde with the legs that went on forever in front of me. She didn't interrupt once, and I was again reminded that I should start talking to people about things instead of trying to bottle them up all the damned time.

When I finished, I took a long drink from my soda and asked, "Well, that do you think?"

"I think I can't believe you've been holding out on me for months, Becca! We've talked about you and this holding everything in thing. It's going to give you a stroke, you know."

"I know, I know. I just didn't want to explain the whole Zane thing and how we knew one another before and everything. I wasn't sure about him. That's the only reason I kept things from you."

Amy smiled and patted my arm. "Relax,

Becca. It's fine. I understand. But you know what I always say. A leopard can't change his spots. That man is obviously no good, honey."

I nodded and reclined back in my chair, feeling slightly more relaxed now that I had gotten this whole Zane thing off my chest. Amy just stared and waited with those big brown eyes of hers as I said, "Even with all the changes I was beginning to see?"

I wanted so badly to believe that the front desk clerk, Mandy, had been right about me having a positive effect on Zane. It seemed like such a silly thing to get my self-confidence wrapped up in, but it meant something to me to know that he had been trying, especially if it was for me.

After blinking a few times and shaking her head, causing her dark curls to bounce to and fro, Amy said with all her cynical heart, "So now we're acting under the impression that men can be changed? Honey, they're going to take away your feminist card. People don't change. They just get worse as they get older. You and I both know that. And the idea that a man can be changed, I mean, come on now."

"But what if he was a good guy underneath all that bad guy stuff?"

Even I knew how sad that sounded as soon as the words left my mouth. When did I become such a pathetic romantic?

Amy just shook her head. If she was judging me harshly, she was kind enough to keep most of it inside as she answered, "He must be pretty damn incredible in bed if you're willing to make all these excuses for him."

"He is," I admitted as I felt my cheeks heat up. "I wish to God he wasn't, but that man is incredible between the sheets."

Amy nodded wisely like an old sage. "I see. That's what this is all about. You're being ruled by your hormones. You need to start thinking with your head, girl."

"I don't know. I don't. At first, I thought he was an ass like he was back when, and then as time went on, he seemed to get nicer, and I guess I began to think maybe we could be together like we were when we were happy before. Then I saw him with that woman and everything that happened all came rushing back. I hated how I felt, but I was jealous."

Amy looked at me with skepticism in her dark eyes. "I don't know what to say other than go with your gut. It's never done you wrong, so go with what it's telling you now."

Go with my gut. Too bad my gut remained tied up in knots, even now days after seeing Zane with another woman.

"You've got this, Becca. No matter what, no

guy gets to bring you down. You know that."

"I know. I guess I just needed to hear it from someone else," I said quietly.

She smiled and gave my arm a sympathetic squeeze. "I better get back out to my desk. You want to go out for a drink after work tonight?"

The pounding in my head made her offer sound perfectly awful, so I smiled and begged off. "Another time. But thanks."

"Anytime, honey. My shoulder's always here for you."

She left me sitting there knowing full well that her advice on following my gut had been right on the money. If I had listened to it in the first place when it was telling me that nothing had changed in Zane, none of this would have happened.

God, I really was stupid when it came to him.

CHAPTER EIGHTEEN

Zane

A FTER A FEW days of not getting a call back from Becca, I decided I needed to up my game. I wasn't going to get her back sitting by the phone pining for her, and there was only one way to truly get her back. So I packed up my car and took off for the city.

I figured it would be nice to escape the judgmental glares of people at the inn anyway. The staff had guessed pretty quickly what had happened, and they'd made it abundantly clear that they all preferred Becca to me by a long shot.

As the miles passed, I realized I hadn't given Becca the credit she deserved. She'd driven all those times to spend working to make sure my business did well. After sitting in traffic for an hour and a half on a highway that resembled a parking lot, raging against whatever construction was holding us up, I realized that alone merited more respect than I had given her, not to mention everything else she'd put up with.

I hadn't been her only client, surely, and she'd been making the trek up from the city to work hard for the inn and me. I'd seen her exploring all the parts of the place and familiarizing herself with the staff, making a real effort to do an amazing job, and I had put her down by letting Stacey come to the one place Becca truly loved.

The music blaring into my car never drowned out the voice in my head that kept reminding me what a total and utter jackass I'd been all those years ago and yet again. I'd had a shot at a terrific woman who seemed to be starting to want me back and what had I done?

I'd bungled it. That's what I'd done.

I tried my best to convince myself that rushing to the city to sweep her off her feet would win her back for sure, but something inside me worried that it wouldn't be enough. That nothing could be enough this time.

She probably thought I'd gone upstairs with Stacey to sleep with her. Of course she did. Why wouldn't she with Stacey hanging all over me like some cheap date?

Fuck. If only I had told Stacey to stay away.

Damn. I didn't want to think about that anymore.

I remembered what she'd said to me that day on the bridge, about what kind of guy I was and how she knew all about my type, and I realized with frustration that she'd been right.

And it was me who'd proven that to her.

I needed to fix my mistake and seeing her was the only way I could do that.

Her business card told me where I had to go, so I headed there. I opened the glass door to her office and saw a woman with curly brown hair sitting at the front desk. She gave me a smile and said, "Hello and welcome to Fox Advertising. How may I help you today, sir?"

Looking around at the comfortable waiting area, I noticed every inch of the place said Becca had been involved in making it welcoming with the brown and white upholstered chairs and matching sofa that made it look more like a living room than an office. The soft scent of lavender that I had come to identify with her floated through the air, and the space felt almost homey with its warm yellow walls.

I smiled back as I approached the receptionist's desk and said, "I'm looking for Becca Fox. Can you tell me where I can find her?"

"I'm sorry, but Becca isn't coming in today. I'd be happy to take any message you would like to leave for her. Otherwise, I can absolutely set up an appointment with her later in the week."

Waiting until later in the week wouldn't do. "I have to speak to her. It's very important," I said, turning on the charm I needed to work on this woman.

"She's not here, sir. I am sorry."

"I know, I believe you. It's just that it's really very important that I speak with her."

"Is this regarding a campaign she's working on for you?" she asked.

"Yes, well, no…I mean…" I stuttered out, not coming off as impressive as I wanted to. "Could you please just give me her home address? It's imperative that I speak with her today."

It was a long shot, and it fell mightily short as she shook her head and frowned. "I'm sorry sir, but I don't even know who you are. I can't give you Becca's home address. It would be unprofessional and unsafe, to say the least. Can you see how it would be wrong to give out someone's address to a stranger who walks in the door and doesn't even look like anyone you've ever seen here before? This is New York, you know."

It would take more charm to get what I wanted, so I turned it on full tilt. Flashing her a smile, I said, "You aren't wrong. I can definitely see that. Becca is lucky to have a good person like you who looks out for her best interests working for her. Hell, I could be some crazy man out to find her to take her kidney or something. What was your name again?"

The woman responded to my compliment with a broad smile. "I'm Amy. I don't want you to think I'm rude or anything, but it just isn't smart to give people's home addresses out to strangers."

Leaning on the edge of her desk, I got down to the receptionist's level so we were eye-to-eye. "I understand. I do. Here's the thing, Amy. I need to see Becca, and I didn't drive all the way down from Vermont to end up this close and not see her. It's very important to me that I see her today. It is hands down the most important thing to me in the world right now, and it needs to happen, come hell or high water."

Amy nodded and appeared to be warming up to me, so I continued. "I can't leave this city without seeing Becca, and if that means I have to sit outside this office until tomorrow morning, I will, but it would probably be a whole hell of a lot more romantic if I showed up at her doorstep. So I'm begging you, will you please give me Becca's address? Please?"

She stared at me like she was considering what I said, and I silently prayed to God that my speech had worked. Little did she know, I had meant every word of it. Well, I would have probably gotten myself a hotel room instead of sitting outside the office all night like some kind of madman, but still, I meant everything else.

"Vermont, huh? That's quite a drive. You must really want to see her."

I sensed at any minute she'd relent and give me what I wanted, so I went in for the kill. "It is, and I wouldn't make it for just anyone. But you know Becca isn't just anyone."

Success!

Amy took out a pen and wrote down the address on a sheet of paper. As she handed it to me, she kept her fingers on one edge, holding it tight between us and narrowing her eyes to a very unfriendly squint.

"I feel like I should tell you that my family knows a lot of people, if you know what I mean. If you go to Becca's house and do anything that isn't incredibly nice and makes her unhappy in the tiniest bit, I'm going to tell my Uncle Tony, and I'm his favorite niece, so he's going to do what I ask him to. You catch my drift, loverboy?"

I stared at her in disbelief, and then out of the corner of my eye I saw her nameplate read Amy Bianchi. Had this woman just threatened to send the mob after me if I did anything to make Becca unhappy?

It was one of those moments where I was glad no one, especially the woman in front of me, could read my mind. I smiled and looked her in the eye as I took the paper from her. "I swear I have no plans to do anything she won't love. The next time you see her, you'll see I did nothing wrong. I swear."

Amy just smiled up at me from her desk and shrugged. "You know what will happen if you don't treat her right. Can't say you didn't have fair warning."

I nodded and left in a hurry, afraid if I didn't that she'd start threatening me with concrete shoes and swimming with the fishes. I put the address in my phone and started heading towards the Upper West Side. Not one block away, however, I encountered the worst bumper to bumper traffic jam I'd ever seen.

Finally, after a grueling hour stuck behind a garbage truck and a school bus, I pulled up in front of her townhouse. The red brick façade made the place look like every Upper West Side of Manhattan townhouse in the movies. It showed the effects of a recent rough winter, but overall, it looked classy and very Becca.

Cream curtains blocked my vision through the front window, but I saw a light and a shadow moving telling me Becca was home. I bounded up the stairs and mentally kicked myself for not thinking to bring some flowers or candy. I needed to start planning ahead better if I ever wanted to successfully woo this woman. I hoped the fact that I was there would be enough as I rang the bell and waited.

A few short seconds later, Becca opened the red front door and stared out at me with a look of shock on her face. "Zane? What...what are you doing here? How did you know where I live? I don't recall giving you my home address at any point," she said hesitantly, not immediately asking me in.

"I went to your job and met a woman named Amy who was nice enough to give it to me after she threatened me with her apparent mob connections if I made you unhappy in any way. Did you know your assistant is some mob boss's niece or something? I know this is New York, but damn, I didn't think everyone was connected like that," I said, beginning to ramble just a bit.

Becca chuckled for a moment before catching herself and pressing her lips together tightly. I liked hearing that from her again and for the moment she smiled, I thought we might be okay.

"Zane, I don't think she is. Well, actually, who knows? Maybe she is connected," she said, her smile fading, along with my hopes that maybe my stupid antics hadn't ruined everything.

"So now that you know that I'm not here to do anything that might endanger my life, can I come in?"

As soon as the words left my mouth, her expression grew dark. "Why? If you're fine with the campaign I have planned, I can begin working on it."

I leaned against the door frame and forced a smile, even as the situation grew worse by the second. "I called you a bunch of times."

She avoided my gaze and looked down the street. "I know."

"Why didn't you call back?" It was a bold thing to ask, and when she snapped her head around to look at me, I saw she knew it too.

I expected to get chewed out right there on her doorstep but Becca, ever the classy one, simply said, "I didn't want to interrupt you and your long-time friend."

Shaking my head, I leaned in toward her. "You wouldn't have interrupted anything. Please, can I come in, Becca?"

"I'm not sure that's a good idea, Zane. Whatever you came here for you could have found out through email. If you have any questions about the campaign, send them to the email address on my business card. I think it would be best if we communicated that way from now on."

Becca stepped back and began to close the door in my face. With every inch it came toward me, I knew my chances to win her over were slipping away. I stuffed my foot in next to the doorjamb, abruptly stopping the door, and took the last opportunity I might ever have to show her

I could be the man she thought I was before I made the mistake of letting Stacey come around.

"Just give me a few minutes. That's all I ask. I just want to talk to you."

She pushed on the door to close it, crushing my foot. Failing to push me out, she looked up at me with hurt in her dark eyes and shook her head. "No, Zane. You disappointed me one too many times in this life. You don't get another chance. Goodbye."

My heart slammed against my chest at the sound of that word coming from her. Goodbye. No! I couldn't let her get away this time. I'd blown it years ago when I was too young and too stupid to deserve her. But now I'd grown up and become a different man.

A better man because of her. I had to make her see that.

Pressing my face into the crack, I began to plead my case. "I'm sorry. I screwed up. Stacey never meant anything to me. The person I was with her doesn't exist anymore. I've changed, and it's all because of you. You made me want to be a better man. Don't let what we can be slip away because I'm an ass. Please, just give me another chance."

Her eyes filled with something I couldn't place. It wasn't hurt anymore, but it certainly wasn't happiness at what she heard from me. I waited for her to say something and braced for another push on the door that would crush my foot.

But she didn't push me away.

Instead, she simply walked into her house, leaving me standing there in the front doorway to her townhouse. Had I succeeded in convincing her to give me another chance?

Or maybe she'd just given up and hoped I'd leave her alone forever.

I couldn't do that, though, so I followed her inside and found her standing in the middle of the hallway with her arms crossed and a look on her face icier than any I'd ever gotten from another human being.

Definitely not the expression of a woman who wanted to hear another word from me.

It didn't matter. All that mattered was I had gotten her to let me in and now she'd have to listen to me. Well, that or the cops would be arriving any minute and I'd be escorted out by New York's finest.

And then she spoke and I knew even if the cops didn't come, I would be facing some punishment for what I'd done.

"So you're going with the better man routine, huh? I made you want to be a better man. What better man would that be, Zanc? Is he better than the man who left me high and dry all those years ago after an incredible day at the pier thinking that something wonderful was happening between us? Is he better than the selfish and thoughtless man who made everyone at the inn hate him? Or is he better than the man who showed up in the dining room of the inn with some bleach blonde bimbo with bought and paid for boobs when he knew I'd be there especially to see him, particularly since I'd just fucking slept with him just seven days before that?"

With every word that left her mouth, her voice grew angrier until she practically spat them out at me. I knew I deserved everything she wanted to throw at me, but to have my bad deeds laid out like that still left me stunned for a moment.

My ego battered, I forced myself to show her that I knew what I'd done and wanted forgiveness for it. "I've been a real fuck, Becca. I don't deny that. But I'm different now."

"Different from the asshole who did what he did just a few days ago with that old friend of yours? What was your goal there, Zane? Did you want me to feel insignificant and ugly compared to Miss Barbie Come To Life? Was that it? Was your male ego too fragile to handle a woman who had more going for her than tits, ass, and the space between her legs?"

The usually sweet natured Becca glared at me

as she hurled her accusations. Something inside my head made me want to defend myself, and before I knew it, the words had left my lips.

"If I remember correctly, you made me feel pretty shitty after we slept together. You barely spoke to me that morning, and you left like even looking at me made you sick. Not exactly the response a guy expects after sleeping with a woman."

Her eyes opened wide with rage, and as regret settled into me, I wondered for a brief moment if I'd be seeing Uncle Tony in the next few days.

"Are you kidding me? If I'm skittish about letting you see how I felt about you, it's only because our past includes you leaving me without even a goodbye after a summer that included the two of us doing things I've only read in books and me sharing things I've never shared with any other person on the planet, Zane. And then you showed me I was right for being afraid to believe that you could ever be anything other than the thoughtless dick you've always been."

Most of what she said didn't seem to offer me much of a chance to win her back, so I seized on the few that could. Stepping toward her, I reached out and touched her on the arm. "You shared things with me that you never did with anyone else? Not even your husband?"

She yanked her arm away and shook her head.

"No way! I'm not letting you do this to me, Zane Gilford. Go back to your fuck toy of a friend you've known a long time and leave me alone."

"I don't care about her, Becca. I care about you. She's nothing compared to you. I know I made a mistake parading her in front of you like that, but I see now that she never meant anything to me. I need you to believe that."

Her mouth dropped open for a moment, and she stared at me in disbelief through narrowed eyes. "It's always about you, isn't it? You need. What do you think I needed?"

I searched for the right words to explain to her what I thought she needed from me, but none of them sounded very convincing. They all made me seem like the same selfish, egotistical asshole she saw me as.

With anger seething from her, she snapped, "See? You've never even given what I needed a single moment's thought. Why would you, right? All you can ever see is what you need."

She spun on her heels and began to walk away from me, but I grabbed her by the wrist to keep her there. If I didn't say the words now, I might never get the chance, so I didn't hold back.

As she stared up at me in shock that I wouldn't let her go, I said what a man fighting to keep the woman he loved with him would say. "You needed to believe in me, and I fucked up.

There it is. The whole truth. You needed to believe that I could be a good man who gave even two shits about the people around me. You wanted me to not be the person who left you that summer day, tossing his things into the back of his car and driving out of town without even saying goodbye. You wanted me to be the person you spent all those days and nights with that summer, that guy who let himself feel for you before he got scared and ran away."

Becca lowered her head and quietly said with a sob, "Don't. Don't stand here and make me think there's someone decent inside you. I won't let you make a fool of me again. I won't."

I stepped forward and tilted her head up to see tears filling her eyes. How many times had she cried because of me? I had to make her see I could be the man she wanted.

The man she needed.

"It's not foolish to believe in someone. If anyone's the fool, it's me. I've been nothing but a jackass to you every time you got close. That's all my fault, Becca. But I'm here because I want you to know I am that person you believed I was."

As a tear streamed down her cheek, she asked a question that made my heart skip a beat. "How can I believe you? You've shown me who you are time and again. How could I ever believe you, Zane?"

I had no answer for that. No matter what I

said, she could point to my actions that always spoke louder than my words. She wasn't wrong. I was that asshole who had broken her heart.

And there was not a damn thing I could do to change that.

"You can't."

I turned and walked toward the door, exhausted from the realization that everything I'd done up to that moment meant more than the words I could use to promise her I could be the man she wanted. I'd spent my life being a selfish asshole, and for the first time, I saw how much it hurt everyone around me.

From behind me, I felt Becca touch my hand. I turned around and saw the true effect of my behavior on the woman I loved. She stared up at me with red-rimmed eyes from crying and a frown that made me hate myself because I'd put that there.

I'd made that beautiful face of hers look that way.

"Don't leave."

"Why would you want me to stay, knowing all the mistakes I've made?"

"Because I'm a fool. I can't help believing in you, Zane," she said quietly, squeezing my hand.

I cradled her face in my hands and kissed her long and deep like I'd wanted to for so long. She wasn't the fool. I was.

But I could change.

CHAPTER NINETEEN

Becca

RIGHT THERE, IN the middle of my front hallway, he lifted me in his arms and carried me up the stairs. When we reached the top, he looked around and smiled.

"I just realized I have no idea where I'm taking you. Point me in the direction of your bedroom, or accept that I might choose the guest room where you have the bad mattress."

I chuckled and stuck my arm out toward the room at the front of the house. "How did you know I do that with the mattresses?"

He began walking again and laughed at my confession. "Because everyone does. You're not going to keep the bad mattress for yourself, are you?"

Burying my head in the space between his jaw and his shoulder, I nodded. "True. But I never said that."

As he pushed my bedroom door open with his

foot, he kissed my cheek. "Don't worry. I'm not planning on remembering that part of this anyway."

Either was I. All I wanted to remember was how this man made me feel when he did things to my body that no other man had ever come close to.

He sat me down on the bed and knelt before me to remove my knee-high black leather boots I'd worn to work that morning. With his eyes locked on mine, he slowly lowered the zipper, his fingers caressing my calf as he moved toward the bottom. Then he carefully lifted my foot out and moved to the other leg to do exactly the same thing. When he finished, he ran his hands up my legs until they rested on my thighs and smiled.

"I love and hate those boots."

"Why?" I asked, confused since I thought the world of them.

"Well, I'm all about stiletto heeled, black leather boots, but if you're wearing them, you're hiding one of your best parts. Or two of your best parts, depending on how you think of it."

I rolled my eyes at his brand of compliment, secretly loving it more than he could ever know. "Well, they're off now."

Zane pushed his hands up higher underneath my skirt to where my legs met my body and sighed. "Your legs were the first things I noticed on you that night at the party. You were wearing those white sandals that made your legs look incredible."

My memory of that night included nothing about what shoes I wore. All I remembered of that night was sex with Zane.

"And as soon as I saw the rest of you, I had to talk to you before some other guy beat me to it," he said in a husky voice as he stood up and pulled his shirt up over his head.

I gazed up at him and my core clenched at how much I wanted him. Reaching up, I clamped my hand onto the waist of his pants to pull him down on top of me. He let me take him down and kissed me long and deep, sending a jolt of electricity straight to my pussy.

Moving his hand up my thigh, he touched my tender clit and rubbed in tiny circles for a moment before sliding a finger into me. I loved the feel of it, but I wanted something else more.

While he fucked me first with one finger and then with two, I opened his pants and slipped my hand inside his boxer briefs to palm his thick cock. Already hard, he moaned into my mouth when I began stroking him slowly from the base to the thick, swollen head.

"I was going to go down on you, but if you keep doing that, I'm going to just skip straight away to fucking you," he said in a low voice next to my ear.

Gripping him tightly, I pumped his cock to encourage exactly what he said. "As much as I love your mouth, I want you inside me more."

I didn't have to say another word. He pulled my skirt and panties down my legs and tossed them on the floor before stripping out of his pants.

He stood there looking down at me as I wriggled out of my top, and when I was naked, he grinned and flipped me over on my stomach. Leaning down, he pressed his cock against my ass and groaned in my ear, "Up on your knees. I'm going to give you exactly what you want."

I did as he commanded and got up on all fours. Wiggling my ass, I turned around to glance at him at the very moment he pushed his hips forward and filled me up completely in one hard thrust that took my breath away. I hung my head and closed my eyes, reveling in the feel of him possessing me, fucking me with abandon as I tightly grasped the bedspread in my hands.

His fingers sunk into my skin and his hands held my hips tightly as he fucked me as perfectly as I'd ever been in my life. I loved the feel of his cock filling me, and knowing he controlled our lovemaking entirely excited me more than I wanted to admit.

Whatever this man had, he possessed me body

and soul. As terrifying as that had always sounded, at that moment when he grunted behind me and moaned my name, I wanted nothing more in life.

My body careened toward the edge, and I tumbled over as an earth-shattering orgasm overtook me, making my legs buckle beneath me. I only remained on my hands and knees because Zane snaked his arm around my waist and held me tight. I pushed back against him while my body surrendered to him completely.

"Oh, God...oh...baby..." he groaned as he came hard, filling me up.

Dropping my head, I rode his release until he moved back away from me and I crashed to the bed, exhausted from being thoroughly fucked. When I finally caught my breath, I rolled over and saw him collapse onto the bed next to me.

I lay breathless and in awe once again at the effect Zane had on me. He kissed me lightly on the neck, and it felt tender and open, something I wasn't entirely accustomed to when it came to him. He spent so much time maintaining that visage of a confident and cocky guy that open felt strange.

Although he still retained some of his cocky self, sex had been different than the time we slept together at the inn. I didn't feel so much like a conquest or a booty call. This time he gave as much as he took. Zane had made an effort to seek me out and pursue me, and that felt good, especially since while he excelled at the pursuing, he'd never been very good at the giving part.

His hands moved to my hips, and I smiled at him. "You're going to have to give me a second there. I'm still recovering from what you just did to me."

He playfully pouted before he nodded and rolled over, pulling me onto his chest. I didn't feel the same need to be guarded and distant with him like I had back at the inn.

"Fine, fine, but I thought maybe a change of position would make you see things my way," he said, winking at me as I looked up to kiss him.

Against his lips, I whispered, "I promise as soon as I regain my strength I'm all for whatever you have in mind."

We lay there in blissful happiness for a few minutes, my head on his chest gently rising and falling in time with his breathing, before he broke the silence. "You know, my mother left me the inn in her will with one specific provision," he said.

I waited for him to continue as I ran my hand up and down his chest. I sensed what he had to say troubled him.

"If I want to collect my inheritance, I have to leave the inn in the same or better condition than it was operating at when she left it to me. I have one year to get through, and then that's it."

I nodded and wondered if that meant after a year he'd been leaving to go back to California.

"It scares me, you know. I don't know if I can keep it at the standard she did. She really loved that place. She loved it like you love it, Becca. I wish I could love it that much too. I just don't think it's for me. I mean, I just can't seem to find the allure in like you do. Maybe it's because I grew up there. I don't know," he said before trailing off, lost in his own memories.

I watched his expression darken, not knowing exactly what to say as a new worry cropped up in my mind. Was the inn the only thing holding us together, or was there something between us that hadn't been there before?

Finally, after a long pause, I said, "Zane, I think you're capable of so much more than you give yourself credit for. Your mother believed in you, and I do too. I've already seen a marked difference from when I first saw you there. I think you're doing a great job and you might not know it, but your staff does too. I've talked to them, and they see the change in you too. You can do this. I know you can."

He didn't say anything in return, and for a long time, we just lay there. Unfortunately, that question in my mind pressed its way forward, and the bliss couldn't last forever. I tried my best to push it away, but the curiosity got to me.

"Zane, all those years ago, why didn't you say goodbye? Why didn't you actually break up with me?"

His body tensed up against mine, and he eased me off him as he muttered something about needing to go to the bathroom. I pointed him in the right direction, but when he came back, I decided I needed to press the issue. I deserved an answer, even if it was ancient history. I couldn't truly move forward with him if I never got an answer, and the longer we put that conversation off, the longer it would stay in my mind.

"Zane, I want to talk about this."

"Well, I don't."

He climbed back into bed next to me, but a noticeable distance existed between us. I wasn't going to let him off the hook that easily. I could understand not living in the past, but some things simply needed to be answered and accounted for.

I shifted the sheets off me as I sat up and looked down at him. "Zane, you need to talk to me. It isn't fair of you to do this, and you and I both know it."

He shook his head. "I just wasn't ready for anything serious back then, okay? I was young and stupid. We all were at one point."

His words stung since I had thought that we were headed somewhere serious back then. It was amazing how old wounds could be opened so easily, and my pride hurt, despite him clearly wanting to move past the issue.

"Is this going to just be a repeat of what we were back then, and what we weren't, apparently? Are you just trying to sleep with me until I show some real interest only for you to back away? It hurt enough the first time, you know."

He stood up out of my bed and pulled his pants on as he crossed the room to the armchair in the corner. Running his hand through his hair like he always did when he was frustrated, he sat down and said, "Are you kidding me? Why the hell would I drive all the way from Vermont just for a lay, Becca? Is that what you think of me?"

I pulled on the white silk robe that I kept on the side of my bed and stared him down. "How else should I think of you? What evidence, other than a few tanks of gas, have you given me to support your claim that you're really any different? I know you've been better with the inn, but that inn isn't what we're talking about right now. You have to be open and honest with me, even about the stuff we don't want to get into. It's important, and you have to know that."

His eyes flashed with anger as he pounded his fist on my window sill, startling me. "Damnit, Becca. What do I need to do to show you that I'm trying to be a better man for you? I'm here, aren't

I?"

"Yes, but for how long this time, Zane? Until you get bored of me or too scared to commit to anything real and run off to California again with that blonde you like so much?"

I usually didn't go for the catty and jealous comment, but he deserved it. I wasn't entirely wrong, after all.

The anger in Zane's eyes turned to sadness, though, and he took a deep, steadying breath before saying, "You want the truth, Becca? You really want to know why I ran away?"

"Of course, I do. You owe me that much at least for breaking my heart. I can't trust you fully if I never really know why you left the first time."

Hanging his head, he said quietly, "You were out of my league. You were in college going for your degree. I wasn't. I didn't even have the prospect of one since school wasn't in my plan. You had a perfect future mapped out, and you succeeded at all of it. I would have held you back. I was just some dumb guy with no plan and no prospects other than my mother's eventual inheritance. I was a nobody, and you were set to conquer the world. I couldn't handle it."

As he finished, I stood there stunned. I had never considered anything like that could have been the reason why he hadn't wanted me.

I padded across the room and knelt down in

front of him, placing my hands on the top of his thighs. "Zane, I never thought of you that way. You weren't some loser with no degree to me. I was falling for you. Hard. I never cared about anything as silly as all that. I was crazy about you, and when you backed away from me with no explanation, it broke my heart.

He took my face in his hands and looked deep into my eyes. "I can never take back what I did, Becca. I wish I could. I'm so sorry that I ever made you feel anything but adored and cared for. I swear to you, though, I'm a different man now, and I cannot wait to prove that to you."

"I want to believe you, Zane. I do. I always have."

"You can. I promise. You'll see."

He punctuated his pledge with a deep and passionate kiss, and without another word I was back to being wrapped in his arms and under the sheets with him. For the first time in a long time, I felt we were back to where we had been years ago, and I couldn't have been happier. He'd truly opened up to me and told me the truth in his heart, and just like that, the pain of the past seemed to evaporate into the bliss of the present.

CHAPTER TWENTY

Zane

BEFORE LONG, OUR time in bed had to end since the real world demanded both of us return to it. I would have been able to stay with her naked between the sheets for the rest of time, but her advertising business and the inn made that impossible.

As Becca rushed around dressing in her work clothes, I sat on the chair and marveled at how incredible this woman truly was. Even hopping across the floor trying to get her shoes on as she ran a makeup brush over her face, she couldn't have been more beautiful.

"You know, I think you might kill yourself if you don't slow down."

She twisted her face into a grimace that didn't diminish her beauty one bit and stopped moving for a moment. "I have a nine-thirty appointment with a company that could be a huge campaign for me, and as much as I'd love to slow down and take in the very appealing scenery of you sitting there in a towel, I'm trying not to be distracted by your pecs and abs, so how about you get dressed?"

"I'm going to take that as a compliment," I joked.

Becca walked over to me and leaned down so our faces were just an inch away from one another. "I'd stay here and ride you like a wild woman if I could, but I can't, so if you don't want to help me ruin a chance for me to land the biggest account of my career, please put some clothes on."

Since I didn't want to ruin her career, I stood up and kissed her long and slow. Pulling away, I saw the smile on her face and liked how it felt making her happy. "Your wish is my command. I'm not insulted at all that the woman I just spent the last day with pleasuring her now wants me to cover up. Not insulted in the least."

She giggled and pushed me toward the bed where my clothes lay. "I promise I'll make it up to you at a future date. You have my word."

I grabbed my pants and slid one of my legs into them. "I'm going to hold you to that."

At the front door, we kissed goodbye, and I didn't want to leave. For the first time in my life, I wished I could stay right where I was.

The whole drive back I couldn't get her out of my head, and I wore a grin a mile wide. When I arrived, the staff walked around like on eggshells, probably because I was so quiet. However, it wasn't anger that was keeping me silent when I came back.

It was determination.

I arrived in Vermont with a newfound drive and a laser focus to make the inn succeed in a way my mother had never dreamed of. I wanted Becca to see my actions matched my words, and the best way to do that was to throw my weight behind the ad campaign and make the place take off.

✧　✧　✧

THROUGHOUT THE WINTER, I watched as Becca's ideas made The Gilford House Inn the destination everyone wanted to go to in New England. I watched as the inn became booked solid for months. Even a travel magazine came to do an article on how the place had taken off, calling it "world renowned." I didn't know if I'd ever describe the inn like that, but its success felt good.

And I had only one person to credit for that.

My staff knew that too. Although they seemed to like me more than before, they loved seeing Becca whenever she came to stay.

Before I knew it, winter gave way to spring. I awoke one day and glanced at the calendar only to realize that I had less than four months left in my year-long stint at the inn. I smiled as I rolled over and looked at Becca, who stayed at the inn with me every weekend for months now. Tired from the drive up the night before, she brushed me off when I nudged her awake and fell right back asleep, her eyes not even opening as she mumbled into her pillow that she wasn't ready to start the day yet.

I left her lying there, her dark hair splayed out on the pillow as she slept, and walked downstairs to check on the inn. As had become the new norm, the dining room bustled with people getting their breakfast and others in the check-in area getting ready to go on the nature tour or the downtown tour Becca had organized for the warmer weather.

The tour guides waved at me, and a couple of the guests on their way into the dining room stopped to talk to me. It took me a moment to realize that it was my mother's lawyer, Mitchell Worthington, and his wife standing before me.

"Mr. Gilford, I must say things are looking quite splendid here! My wife and I saw your ad in the local paper, and we're glad we booked early."

I smiled, happy to once again hear that Becca's efforts had done so well. "Hello, Mr. Worthington. I'm so happy to see we were able to fit you in. The advertising campaign has really done wonders."

He shook my hand and nodded. "Your mother would be so proud. I don't think I even saw it this busy when she ran the place, and those were what we thought were the salad days of The Gilford House Inn. You certainly have defied all of our expectations. Congratulations, my boy."

"Thank you. I appreciate that."

They walked into the dining room, and I immediately turned to Mandy standing at the check-in desk. "I want to make sure the Worthingtons' meals are comped. Please make sure you handle that before they get their bill at the end of their stay, okay?"

"My pleasure, Mr. Gilford," she answered with a big smile.

I didn't know if she liked me any more than she ever had, but lately it seemed she liked how I ran the inn more than when I first arrived. That wasn't a huge challenge, though. I had pretty much been public enemy number one for a while there.

It still felt a little strange when guests waved and smiled at me as they passed by. Becca had come up with the idea that The Gilford House Inn name needed a face put to it, so now because of the campaign, people recognized me all over the place. It wasn't just at the inn either, where at least it made sense.

One day shortly after the ads started running, I drove into town and everywhere from the grocery store to the shops on Main Street, people walked right up to me and asked if there were any bookings available at my inn. My inn. I didn't often admit it, but I loved it.

A crush of guests stood in front of Mandy at the check-in desk, so I hopped on the second computer I had installed and took charge, helping her through every one of them and clearing out the lobby.

When we finished and the crowd left, she smiled at me and said, "Thank you so much, Mr. Gilford. I didn't mean to start falling behind, but when they all start talking at once like that, it just gets so crazy!"

I nodded my understanding, happy to help. "Don't worry, Mandy. You were doing just fine. I think maybe I should look into hiring another front desk clerk to assist you up here."

Instantly her smile faded, and worry settled into her eyes. "Would I lose my hours? I just started some college courses, and financial aid isn't going to cover all of it. I need my hours, Mr. Gilford. I promise that I won't fall behind like that again. Just please don't take my hours away."

"Mandy, no need to worry. You wouldn't lose any hours, and besides, as the front desk manager, you should be getting a raise anyway for all you do."

She beamed at the news, and for a moment I thought she might just hug me.

"Oh, my God, Mr. Gilford! That would be amazing. I...I can't even... That would be so great! I could afford my rent easier and still have money for school. That would just mean so much to me!" she said, bubbling with joy.

"We'll talk about it next week and nail down some of the specifics. Get me your class schedule so I can have that in mind when looking for someone new, and let me know what you think your salary should be and we'll negotiate from there. Sound good?"

"Yes. Thank you so much, sir."

I waved her off and left the lobby area pleased with myself. It would be good for a young girl like that to start getting some managerial experience. As the only one in the place who'd had the guts to stand up to me, I knew she could handle people working under her. I hadn't forgotten that talk we'd had months before, and I doubted she had either. She might not have known it, but she'd motivated me to get Becca back that day. For that alone, she deserved a raise and a promotion.

Feeling good, I headed back to my room to find Becca in the shower. I walked in and stripped before sneaking in behind her. She jumped with a start but quickly melted into my arms as I lathered soap onto her gorgeous body.

"NICE WAY TO give a girl a heart attack," she said with a smile, gazing up at me as my hands slid over her ass.

"Can't have that happening. I don't want to have to explain this to the local EMTs. If you survived, you'd never be able to show your face in town again. You'd be the shower hussy," I said with a chuckle as her eyebrows shot up into her forehead.

Becca took my cock in her hand and began stroking it, sending a jolt of pleasure through me. "Shower hussy? I'll show you hussy."

A few more strokes made me want much more than just her hand, so I kissed her hard and lifted her so I could slide into her tight cunt. Becca grabbed hold of my shoulders and I pushed into her, loving how every inch of her felt.

"Oh, God," she moaned. "God, fuck me."

Happy to oblige, I gently pressed her back against the white tiles and held her hips tightly before I began to pump into her. Becca loved to take very hot showers, and the hot water continued to hit my shoulder and side, stinging my skin, but I didn't care.

All I cared about was burying my cock inside her cunt and making her come. Her fingers slipped from their hold on my shoulder, so she stuffed them into my hair and tugged hard to hold on as every thrust into her inched her closer to release.

"Oh…Zane…I'm so close…don't stop. Just a few more…"

Her voice trailed off, and closing her eyes, she winced as her cunt began to milk my cock through her orgasm and she tugged harder on my hair. The pain dancing across my scalp and a few tight squeezes around my cock pushed me over the edge, and seconds later, I came, exploding into her and filling her up.

I pressed my forehead to the cool tiles and exhaled, realizing I'd been holding my breath the whole time I made love to her. Becca gently ran her hands over my back as her legs loosened from around my waist.

"That was incredible. I think I almost passed out," she said in my ear.

The hot water pelting my left shoulder suddenly felt like burning coals, and I turned her around to stand under the spray as I lowered her to the tub. Looking down at my skin, I saw a bright red patch.

"I think I have second-degree burns, but it was worth it."

She cradled my face in her hands and stood on her toes to kiss me on the lips before placing a kiss on my shoulder. "All better now."

"I'll leave you to it so I can find some burn ointment," I said with a chuckle. "See you in a few. Don't stay too long in that water or your skin is going to turn to leather."

THE WEEKENDS HAD become the most important part of my weeks, and as I sat in the dining room with Becca watching her eat while I finished my own breakfast, I couldn't help but smile wide. She looked up at me and her cheeks turned red.

"What? Zane, what? Is there something in my teeth?"

"No. I'm just very happy."

She smiled back and gave me a peck on the cheek as I heard screaming coming from the other end of the dining room. We both turned quickly, and I saw a woman sitting at a corner table decked out in all the jewelry and fur one could imagine and yelling at one of my servers. I waited for a moment, seeing if the girl could handle it, but I saw the tears welling up in her eyes.

"Are you an idiot?" the woman shouted, causing the entire dining room to stop and notice her.

She didn't seem to care and continued barking at the poor girl. "I asked for sweet tea. Sweet tea! This doesn't have anything in it. This is the second time this week this has happened. What exactly am I paying for if not some decent service and my preferred type of tea? Is it so hard to get it right?"

I looked at Becca before getting up and walking over to the woman and my server, a girl named Renee who had just started a few weeks earlier. "Hello, ma'am. My name is Zane Gilford, and I'm the owner. What can I do for you today?"

"You can hire some decent staff who can do more than sticking their thumb up their ass and sing. How hard is it to get some sweet tea here?"

"Ma'am, I'm sorry for the inconvenience. I'll be happy to get you some sweet tea. That being said, I can't have you degrading my staff the way you are."

The woman's eyes opened wide in shock that I'd said that to her. As I stood there waiting for her to apologize, it occurred to me at that moment that just a few short months ago I was the one speaking to my staff like that. Disgust for how rude I'd been made me cringe.

The garish woman shook her head and cleared her throat. "Excuse me? I can talk to whoever I like however I want. I paid to be here so if you don't value that…"

Before she went any further, I needed to show that I'd learned my lesson. "I do value that and I value your patronage, but I value my staff as well.

Renee here doesn't deserve to be berated by you or anyone else in this world. Now let me get that sweet tea for you."

I left her fuming and motioned for Renee to follow me as I walked to the server area where two other waitresses stood watching the entire scene.

She hung her head and began to cry. "I'm sorry, Mr. Gilford. I didn't mean to mix up the teas. This is all my fault."

"Renee, it's fine. It's tea. I'll bring this back to her. Why don't you take a break and cool down? Ladies, can you cover her tables for her?" I said as I patted Renee on the shoulder.

She lifted her head and wiped her cheeks stained with mascara from the tears she'd been crying over the obnoxious woman. "I appreciate that Mr. Gilford. Thank you. I'll just take a walk outside to catch my breath. I'll be back in a few minutes."

The other servers consoled her and went back into the dining room behind me as I walked the sweet tea over to the woman. The rage came off of her in waves as I set the drink down with a smile.

"Here you go, ma'am. Is there anything else I can get for you today?"

"Where did you send that little idiot?" she growled at me, looking around for her victim, clearly not done taking her anger out on the girl.

I stood looking down at her pretty damn

stunned that she wouldn't let this go. It was just tea, for fuck's sake.

"Ma'am, I'm going to have to ask you again to mind your tone in my establishment. We don't tolerate rudeness to the staff here."

Her mouth dropped open and she snapped, "You know what? You can get me a refund, you ass. I'm leaving. I won't spend another night in a place that can't be run the right way."

"As you wish, ma'am. I'll take care of you at the front desk—"

She stood up from her chair and threw her napkin down on the table. "Forget it! I only have one night left anyway. Keep my money. I won't spend another minute here."

And with that, the woman stormed out of the dining room. Shrugging, I heard the people at the tables all around the dining room applaud. I smiled and nodded, a little embarrassed that they had to sit through such a show, before taking my seat next to Becca, who was clapping loudest of all.

"Babe, that was amazing! You put her right in her place," she said as she planted a kiss on my cheek. "I'm going to be honest," she whispered. "That was pretty sexy."

I grinned and kissed her back. "That's me. Sexy bed and breakfast owner and soon to be on the receiving end of the world's worst Yelp review."

"Well, I mean it. I thought it was pretty hot."

"You know, it hit me that I was that person not too long ago. I can't believe I ever treated people like that."

Becca looked around and gestured to my staff who were all looking at me appreciatively as Renee came back in to continue her shift. "I think they've forgiven you for that, Zane. You've really changed, and I'm so impressed."

"Oh, yeah?" I asked as I leaned over toward her. "Impressed enough to come back upstairs and waste a little of the day away together?"

She blushed and pursed her lips. "Aren't you needed around here, boss man?"

I swiveled my head back and forth and saw my staff doing a great job handling the guests. "Are you kidding me? These guys have it under control. I can take a little time away."

"Not too little time, I hope," Becca said as she stood and winked at me.

Following behind her toward the staircase that led to my room, I felt my cock get hard at the promise of being inside her again. As I walked up the stairs, checking out her beautiful ass and gorgeous legs in front of me, I smiled to myself.

Life was good.

CHAPTER TWENTY-ONE

Becca

LOOKING FORWARD TO another weekend up in Vermont with Zane, I packed up my briefcase and prepared for my drive to what had become my favorite place on earth. Amy came into my office for our end-of-day meeting before I headed out.

"You going back up there to be with that sexy man again this Fourth of July weekend?" she asked with a sly grin.

"Yup. It's my second home now, I suppose. My little retreat with Zane. You aren't going to call your made up mob boss uncle on us are you?" I teased her.

She shook her head and chuckled. "Uncle Tony? Not as long as Zane stays as this wonderful guy who obviously is making you happy."

I closed my briefcase and looked at her, suddenly realizing that I'd been so wrapped up in work and Zane that I hadn't even talked to Amy much this past week. "You know, you can come with me if you want. I'm sure Zane wouldn't mind, and I doubt all the rooms are booked up. It is the slow season."

Amy shook her head. "And crash your romantic weekend? I'll pass. I've got plans with a surgeon I met at an art gallery downtown last week. He's blond, and I know how we feel about blond men. They can't be trusted, but you've given me hope, so I'm testing the waters."

Grabbing my bags, I walked around my desk and gave her a hug. "I want to hear all about it on Tuesday when I get back from the holiday off. If there's a trustworthy blond man out there, you better believe I want the details."

"Oh, you will, and in excruciating detail to boot," she said with a laugh as she waved me off. "Go. I know you're itching to see Zane. I'll come up with you at some point, hopefully before you guys end up marrying one another there. Enjoy your Fourth!"

My cheeks warmed from a blush, and I couldn't think of a response as she stuck her tongue out at me, so I just rolled my eyes and stepped out into the city and headed towards my car. Before I knew it, the long drive was past me, and Zane stood on the front porch of The Gilford House Inn waiting for me with a smile.

He took my bags and kissed me softly on the

lips. "I'm glad you're back. It was a hell of a week here without you."

Not only was he kind and attentive, but he also seemed to really be loving the inn too. I hadn't said a word to him about it, but I hoped that he'd decide to keep it after the year ended. I loved it there, and although I hadn't committed to a life with him or anything like that, I wouldn't have minded one bit spending the rest of my days in that cozy escape in the Vermont mountains.

The town the inn sat above showed off its patriotism for the Fourth of July holiday with flags and red, white, and blue bunting on nearly every front porch on Main Street. We watched the annual Independence Day parade standing on the cobblestone sidewalk and the smell of barbecue hung thick in the air. I'd never celebrated the Fourth in a small town like this, and on our walk back up to the inn, we bought ice cream cones at Double Dips, the ice cream parlor owned by the twin sisters Jenna and Kenna Samuels.

When we arrived back at the inn, Zane directed me away from the house and toward the woods. "I have a surprise for you."

"What is it?" I asked impatiently as we walked to a spot set up with a picnic for two in an area surrounded by trees.

He stopped and held out his hand. "I just

want to tell you how much I love when you're here."

We sat down on a blanket on the ground, and he poured me a glass of wine. Taking it, I said, "Zane, I can't even explain how wonderful these last few months have been."

"You don't need to. I feel the same way."

Looking at the gorgeous scenery around me, I turned toward him and saw the man who had really become the world to me. "It's been like a dream. The whole week in the city I'm just waiting to come back here."

Zane smiled and clinked his glass to mine. "How is the Mafioso doing?"

I couldn't help but laugh. "I still can't believe you fell for that. You do realize that just because someone in New York has an Italian name doesn't mean they're in the mob, right?"

He shrugged and chuckled. "Of course, but it doesn't mean they aren't. You can't be too careful in this world, Becca. Besides, she was very convincing."

We ate and drank in that grove until the sun began to go down, leaving a trail of orange and red across the sky as it settled behind the mountains. Leaning over, Zane whispered, "I love spending all this time with you. I do."

"I can't think of anywhere else I'd rather be," I said as I sat wrapped in his arms. "I wish I could stay here forever."

It felt more right than ever before between the two of us. Even the time we spent together in California hadn't felt as perfect as now. We remained there as night fell until mosquitos chased us back to the inn.

Rushing through the front door, we headed toward the stairs. "Keep an eye on everything for me, will you, Mandy?" he called to the front desk clerk as I giggled and he chased me up the stairs to our room.

"Aye aye, captain!" I heard her call back as I hit the first stair landing.

Zane might not have realized it, but it warmed my heart to hear the staff be so fond of him. Mandy and I had talked the weekend before, and from what she told me, Zane had turned into the best kind of boss and a totally different man. She'd been practically glowing when she described his behavior.

Three other staff members had rushed over to confirm what she was telling me, going on and on about how he not only had become a great boss but had even started taking an interest in their opinions on how to make the inn even better. Best of all, they had all compared him to his mother, something I knew wouldn't have come lightly for a staff that had adored her.

He came into the room and closed the door.

Alone with him, I smiled and took his face in my hands as I kissed him. "It's so great to see you getting along with the staff. I almost don't even recognize this new man you've become, Zane."

Arching his eyebrow, he grinned. "Oh, yeah? I hope not all of me is unrecognizable," he said before bending down and kissing my neck.

I slid my hand down over his muscular abs and dipped my fingertip beneath his pants to tease the tip of his cock. "I think some parts are still very familiar."

Zane tilted his head back and groaned low and deep, making his Adam's Apple bob up and down. "Damn, woman. You're driving me crazy."

"I think you're due for a reward for being such a great boss," I said, unzipping his pants and palming his hard cock.

He looked down at me as I lowered myself to my knees. "Oh yeah? I think you might be right."

Licking my lips, I grinned. "Good."

He gripped his cock at the base and fed it into my mouth, taking command of our sex like I loved. It was thick and hard, but I took every delicious inch in until the swollen head grazed the back of my throat. I didn't try to go faster than the pace he set as he pushed his hips forward slowly and then pulled back, easing out of my mouth.

The whole act made me run wet with desire

for him, and with my free hand, I rubbed my clit through my shorts. My eyes closed, I let myself get lost in the eroticism of him fucking my mouth while I masturbated until I heard him moan, "Uh-uh."

I opened my eyes and saw him shaking his head. Moving my head so his cock popped out, I asked, "What?"

"No playing with yourself. That should be mine."

"Then come down here and take it," I said with a smile.

Without saying another word, he lifted me up onto my feet and stripped me out of my clothes. Then he ripped off my panties, startling me.

"Zane! What are you doing?"

He picked me up into his arms and carried me to the bed. "Taking my reward. Lie down."

I did as he ordered and watched as he stepped out of his pants, not even bothering to take off his shirt before he plunged into me with a single hard thrust. He slowly lowered himself down on top of me, whispering, "God, Becca. You feel so good."

How I adored this man who had claimed my heart so long ago that summer in California! Now that he'd changed to show the rest of the world how incredible he could be, I wanted to spend the rest of my life with him.

"I love you, Zane. I always have," I whispered

in his ear as my body raced toward release.

In my ear, he said in a husky voice the words that made me happier than I'd ever been before. "I love you, Becca."

He made love to me like he did so long ago, in a way that thrilled me and made me feel adored at the same time. I came and then he did moments later, and we lay there in each other's arms, completely satisfied and in no hurry to get back to the rest of the world as fireworks began to explode outside.

This room was our sanctuary. Here, we were just Zane and Becca, two people who had found each other, lost one another, and found each other again.

BY ALL DEFINITIONS, things had become perfect between us. I loved him and he loved me, and I looked forward to what we were building together. Neither one of us had mentioned plans for the future, but we sure acted like we wanted to spend the rest of our lives together.

One day I woke up and Zane had already gotten into the shower. Usually, I would have joined him, but I felt kind of lazy that morning and chose to lay around for a few minutes before I stretched and lazily walked around the room to look outside at the beautiful day that awaited us.

I caught sight of a manila folder on top of Zane's desk and couldn't help but stop and let my curiosity get the best of me. I'd never been a nosy woman, but Zane and I kept no secrets from one another, so I didn't think it would be an issue. I could have interrupted his shower to ask him, but it seemed silly to disrupt the man's moment of peace in the morning.

I opened the folder, and a quick glance of the legal documents told me that Zane planned on selling the inn. With a frown, I set the envelope down, wishing I hadn't given in to my curiosity so I could keep on living with the fantasy that maybe he was going to keep the place after all.

Disappointed, I sat down at the edge of the bed. Not that his selling the inn would be a total deal breaker. A man was allowed to do what he wanted with his life, and the deal had only been to keep the inn for a year. To hold it against him would have been silly and unfair of me.

Zane had to run into town on an errand, so I headed down to the dining room to have some breakfast alone. As I sat there savoring my bacon and eggs like always, Mandy walked in and stopped beside my table, but she didn't look like her usual happy self.

"Everything okay?" I asked as she pulled out a chair and sat down across from me. "You look like you just got bad news. Is everything okay? How's the semester going?"

It surprised me to see her so unhappy since she'd been in high spirits ever since Zane had promoted her to the position of manager, a job she'd taken to naturally and excelled at, as far as he'd told me.

"I'm going to have to look for a new job, and I have no idea where to start. I've worked at The Gilford House Inn forever. I don't know where to begin looking, and it's all just too much right now. None of the other big chain hotels seem to be hiring for anything but maids, and I can't afford to take the pay cut since I signed up for classes already and paid my tuition. It's just a lot to handle right now."

Deidre Gilford had given Mandy her first job at the inn. She'd started her as a cleaning girl and had moved her up to front desk once she'd been old enough. She'd never left, and I admired her loyalty, especially when Zane had been being such a bastard to everyone there in the beginning.

That made her leaving all the stranger, so I asked, "Why do you have to find a new job? I thought Zane was so much easier to work for lately. Aren't you happy here?"

"You don't know, do you?" she asked, her eyes wide with surprise as she shook her head. "I figured he at least would have told you about it."

"Know what, Mandy?" I asked.

"He's selling this place as soon as his time's up. He had to spend one year here, and after that, he gets to inherit all his mother's money because he didn't run the place into the ground," Mandy said with more than a hint of disgust in her voice as she practically spat out the words.

"Oh, I know, but he's not the inn type anyway. I'm sure everyone here will love the new owners," I explained, trying to comfort her.

However, I saw no peace in her eyes, and she continued to shake her head and grimace.

"So you don't know. He's selling the place, and the new owners are firing all of us. They want to start fresh with their own staff that they're bringing from another hotel. We found out yesterday."

Instantly, I was horrified. I couldn't believe what I was hearing. "Does Zane know? We have to tell him. He'll make sure the new owners can't do that to you."

She frowned and shook her head again. "I doubt he even cares. This place was always a means to an end for him. We just never thought it would be the end of all of us too," Mandy said as I saw tears well up in her eyes.

I reached over and squeezed her arm in sympathy. "No. Stop that. We'll get this all figured out. You've seen Zane over the last few months. He's different. You even told me that yourself."

"I know, I know. I just…it's too much."

She shrank away from my touch and rushed out to the front desk. I glanced around the dining room and saw by the sad looks on the staff's faces that they knew their fate too. I couldn't believe this, though. Zane couldn't know what the new owners were planning to do.

He couldn't.

CHAPTER TWENTY-TWO

Becca

IT FELT LIKE Zane took forever to get back as I waited for him on the front porch of the inn. How could he not have told me? He had to be in the dark as to what the new owners planned to do to his staff.

He had to.

I just couldn't believe after all he'd done to become a man everyone respected at the inn that he could just toss aside all the people who'd served his mother and him so loyally. I paced back and forth, wringing my hands, hoping that Zane didn't know the new owners intended to let everyone go and would be as outraged as me.

His car pulled up, and I watched him walk toward the porch wearing that same cocky yet sexy grin I loved. I wanted so much to hold on to the belief that he didn't know what selling the inn meant, but I couldn't dance around the subject.

When he walked up, I point blank asked him,

"Zane, did you know that your selling this inn means everyone will lose their job?"

He stopped in front of me and nodded but said nothing.

"They're planning to fire everyone when they take over and put their people in here. Did you know that? Everyone, and I mean everyone, will have to leave this place and go somewhere new. It's a small town, Zane. I don't think they'll all be able to find jobs very easily"

He stood quietly for a moment, clearly thinking before he spoke, before replying, "Yeah. I know about it. It's part of the deal."

Horrified, I stepped back away from him. "And you're okay with this? All those people who worked here for years, dedicated their lives to your mother's inn, will now just be disposed of after all that? Do you even care about what happens to them, Zane?" I asked, trying to keep my cool but quickly failing.

How could anyone be so dismissive of other people?

Zane leaned in to kiss me, but I simply turned my head. The nerve he had, trying to kiss me when I was trying to discuss something so important with him. These were people whose lives were about to be completely upended.

I pulled away and backed up towards the door as I said, "Please answer the question, Zane. Now.

Are you okay with this?"

Once again, he nodded. Running his hand through his hair, he said flatly, "It's just business, Becca. They want their people to work here. I can't blame them for that. I'm sure all these people will find work. They're good at what they do. I'll be sure to give them all nice references. I won't just leave them high and dry."

His ability to be cavalier with the futures of all those good people who worked so hard for him disgusted me. I took another step backward, putting more distance between us as I felt more and more revolted by his dismissive behavior. These people had given their sweat and, thanks to his attitude and anger at times, tears for The Gilford House Inn. His mother would have never done such a thing, and deep down I think he knew that by the troubled look on his face.

"How kind of you to bother, Zane. You're upending all their lives, but do console your conscience by giving them all nice references. God knows your mother would have put everyone on the street but with nice references, right?"

He stepped forward to close the gap between us and reached out to take me into his arms. "Becca, come on now…"

I couldn't let this just pass, so I stormed off to our room to get my things. I rushed past the check-in desk and up the stairs as tears welled in my eyes.

Selling the place I could have handled. I could have. I'd hoped he would keep the inn, but I could understand him not wanting to.

But the man I had seen on the front porch was far too much like the one who had bailed on me years ago. I truly thought Zane had come to understand that the inn was more than just a place to survive for a year and that the people who worked there were more than just the help, as he used to call them. I thought of the cooks with their funny little pissing contests about who was the better chef. I thought of the maids who quietly but diligently kept the inn in a condition Zane could never handle on his own. Most of all, I thought of Mandy, the sweet college student who had just enrolled in extra credits thanks to her boost in pay and who was so excited to be living in her own apartment, sustaining herself.

It was all just too much. I couldn't tolerate it a second more, so I packed my things in a hurry to get away from the disappointment and hurt that now felt like it had taken over The Gilford House Inn.

Zane caught up to me and closed the door as I stuffed my clothes into my suitcase. "Becca, don't you think you're making a big deal out of something that really isn't that big a deal at all?"

I stopped packing for a moment and looked at

him in shock. "Not a big deal? You're being heartless, and you know it. Where are these people going to work? Have you thought about that at all?"

"It's not like they can't find other jobs. There are other hotels around here. It is Vermont. You've noticed all the other hotels, motels, and bed and breakfasts in the area, right?"

God, he was so thoughtless!

"You're acting like the spoiled brat everyone thought you were until a few months ago. Where's that kind man you've been convincing everyone you are? Where's the guy who told me the other night that he was starting to understand where his mother had been coming from when she spoke of how valuable the staff here was?"

Then the truth dawned on me, and my shoulders sagged. "You already knew at that point that you were selling this place off to the highest bidder regardless of what they were going to do with these people and you said that to me anyway?"

A sheepish look came over his face. "It's just business. That's it."

All the disappointment and hurt I felt from believing in him and once again being wrong spilled out of me, and I didn't try to stop it. "Just business? People aren't just business! What the fuck is wrong with you, Zane? Why is it so easy for you to be such an insufferable dick to people without any regard to how they might feel?" I screamed.

"Enough. You don't get to stand there and claim I'm a spoiled brat and an asshole after everything I've done to change for you. You wanted me to be nice, so I was nice. You wanted me to care, so I cared. Don't look at me now like I'm a bad guy."

"Like what, Zane? Like what you are? You don't care about anyone but yourself. How can you sell this place off and not even care what happens to these people? The people who, by the way, put up with you when you were an insufferable prick to them. The people who tolerated your grumpy and belligerent self before you supposedly changed. Those people earned the right to be treated with more respect than this, and you deny them even an iota of it."

He paced for a minute before choosing his words, but then he turned around and snapped, "You know what, Becca, how is this any of your damned business anyway? I'm sure if I show them how well your ads have worked for the place they'll be happy to give you more work. Is that your worry here? That your precious getaway from your life in the city will be lost forever? You're acting like you're a fucking co-owner here, but you're just..."

He stopped talking and looked away. I waited for him to finish his sentence, but he didn't. So I did.

"I'm just what, Zane? Just the woman who shares your bed?"

Turning to face me, he shook his head. "You don't own this place, and you don't know what it's been like. So how is any of this your business?"

"Are you fucking kidding me? You think that's what this is about? How can you be so self-centered as to think that is what is going on here? And how is it my business? I thought we were moving toward something, but once again, you proved me wrong."

More than angry, I stood there shocked and hurt. I felt tears begin to well in my eyes and struggled to hold them back. Zane wasn't going to see me cry. He was going to see what happened when I walked away from him.

All of a sudden, I felt like I was back in the hallway with that poor maid, back when I had just seen him berating someone over nonsense. It hurt because at that moment I realized he saw me very much like he saw her.

For all that I'd thought we'd become, he'd never changed from that bastard who didn't give a damn about anyone but himself. He truly thought it wasn't any of my business despite the fact that I thought our lives had become intertwined enough that it was our business what the other one was dealing with and going through. I'd told him all about the townhouse issue with Dustin and about every other problem or good thing in my life, and he had been keeping this secret from me.

It hurt, but I wouldn't let him see that inside I felt broken.

And betrayed. Again.

"Becca. I didn't…it's not like that."

I shook my head and backed away from him. "I guess I just thought that we were moving toward a future together and that would mean that the big things in your life were my business," I said, my voice smaller than when I had been yelling but no less defiant.

Jamming more clothes into my bag, I looked around the room for anything I might have forgotten. Now as I glanced at the four walls and everything in there, it all felt foreign, like I didn't belong there.

I picked up my bag and turned toward the door where Zane stood staring at me like he couldn't believe how upset all this made me.

"Becca, don't do this. Don't throw away everything we have together."

"Everything we have together? So were you planning on leaving again? Were you at least going to say goodbye this time or were you just going to drive off into the sunset without a care in the world for the woman who you'd just been sleeping with. I'm so glad that's all you thought I was."

Zane said nothing for a moment, looking at me with sadness in his eyes before saying, "I didn't mean it like that. I swear. I just meant…"

His voice trailed off and then he said, "It wasn't going to be like that. We can be together. I wanted us to be together forever. It just doesn't have to be here."

"You don't get it, Zane. I can't be with someone who is so thoughtless. You're exactly the person you always were. I just convinced myself you'd changed because I wanted you to, but you didn't. You're the same asshole who left me without even a goodbye after all we shared, and I don't want to be with that guy."

He gently touched my arm. "That's not true. What we have is still great. Don't let this ruin it. I'm the man you thought I was. I swear I am, Becca."

"What do we have? You kept this a secret from me because you knew. You knew I'd have a problem with what you're doing because it's not right. It's not the right thing to do, and you know it."

He didn't respond and simply nodded as I pushed past him to leave. After everything, he had nothing to say.

Why should I care? He hadn't changed at all. Everything had been for show, and now that his year at the inn was nearly up, he had no more reason to pretend.

I walked out without another glance at him. Back down the hallway, down the stairs with the one that creaked near the bottom, past the front desk, and out the front door I walked as a feeling of emptiness took me over.

As I started to feel wistful like I always did when I left The Gilford House Inn, I opened my car door and thought back to what Amy had said.

"Leopards don't change their spots."

How right she'd been. I made a mental note to never ignore the advice of a good friend again as I threw my things in the car and drove off, The Gilford House Inn looking sad on its mountain behind me as if to say that it too wanted to go with me.

My phone vibrated over and over, and then it began to ring. Glancing down, I saw every message and call was from Zane. I knew what he wanted to say. That we could still be together and things could be great like they had been for the past few months. That we were more than the inn.

That he loved me.

I so wanted to believe that. To believe Zane was the person I thought he was. To believe that I hadn't let myself fall for him again and been wrong again.

Driving back to the city, I sobbed and grieved the end of the relationship as anyone would, but I had the realization somewhere along the interstate that I should have known better. Nobody changes. Not really. Not unless they want to for themselves. It was a very simple truth that I finally needed to accept.

CHAPTER TWENTY-THREE

Zane

LIFE OFFERED FEW things better than a nice warm day when a man could drive with the top down and enjoy the sun beating down on him as he tore down the highway at top speeds. The rest of the world faded away in those moments, so I knew to take advantage of them when they came along.

The wind caught my hair and rang in my ears, and I turned up the music and pressed my foot on the gas pedal as I looked toward the horizon. I drummed my hands on the steering wheel and bobbed my head to the beat. Things were good, and even though I was alone, the sun and the music were good enough company for me.

Sadly, a phone call interrupted my bliss, and through the speakers I heard, "Mr. Gilford, the attorney called. She needs to speak to you as soon as possible."

"Did she say why?"

"No, but she sounded like things were about to be finalized."

"Fine. Thanks," I said, hanging up before turning my music back up to enjoy the rest of my drive.

When I pulled up to the office, I put the top up and checked my look in the mirror before I strode in, full of good vibes and an even better mood and outlook. The receptionist welcomed me and ushered me into the attorney's office before handing me a glass of water and leaving. An especially efficient attorney, Kristen Jacobs came in a minute later. She had an all-business look with her short blonde bob, glowing tan, and stern expression.

"Good afternoon, Mr. Gilford. I'm glad you could make it in so quickly. I imagine traffic is a nightmare out there at this hour."

"I took the scenic route, so not too bad. Besides the sun is shining, so it's a great day. You should get out of this office and enjoy it. It's days like this that make me want to jump in my car and head for the beach."

She raised an eyebrow and leveled her gaze on me with a look that said she thought my suggestion was ridiculous, but she enjoyed taking my money, so she stayed silent.

Getting down to business, I asked, "Is the paperwork finished?"

She nodded as she pulled a stack of papers from an envelope and pushed them across the desk toward me. "Are you sure you want to do this? That's a lot of money you're leaving on the table."

I scanned the legalese on the papers in front of me and then looked up at her. "You know, I guess I should be more worried about that, but I'm just not."

"Well, we can't easily come back from this point, so you need to be sure, Mr. Gilford. Otherwise, you'll be paying me a lot to get back less. Understand?"

I signed my name where the tabbed arrows directed me to and said, "I know."

The business of the day done, I walked out of the office and enjoyed the warm sun on my face for a moment before I looked around at all the gorgeous trees and breathed deeply. The fresh air filled my lungs and gave me a momentary high I'd never found anywhere but here.

I had to admit I enjoyed Vermont in the fall. The place held a certain peacefulness that even I couldn't deny. I still hadn't fully acclimated to the cold, but the crisp mountain air and colorful foliage were charming in some ways. I hadn't even thought about California in a while and found that I didn't miss it all that much.

As if to remind me why I liked it more than

California, the owner of the coffee shop I frequented walked into the parking lot next to the law office and caught sight of me.

"Zane! Now I know you aren't going to come this close to my shop and not get a cup of joe!" Elaine Taylor said, her gray hair flying in the wind as she rushed over to me.

I smiled and shook my head. "Not today, Mrs. Taylor. You'll have to forgive me," I said, turning on the charm I knew she liked so much.

She smiled and pulled me in for a quick hug. "Word around town is you're keeping that inn of your mother's."

I could tell she was trying hard not to gossip, but she was terrible at hiding her true motives.

"Just signed the paperwork before you caught me. The Gilford House Inn will stay just that. You know there's always room for you if you want to get away for a little while."

"That is so good to hear! Your mother was one of my dearest friends, and she would have been so proud to see all that you've accomplished. Here, let me grab you a cup for the road, okay?"

There was no turning her down, so I nodded and thanked her. She rushed back out a minute later with a cup of coffee made just how I liked it and a donut too.

"You spoil me, Elaine."

"Of course. You deserve it. Now you be good

up on the mountain and remember to call my husband when the snow eventually gets here. He's itching to use that new plow of his."

"I sure will. Have a good one, and thanks for the coffee!"

I walked back to my car and drove the winding road up the mountain to the inn where my staff waited on the front porch all wearing smiles. In the very front stood Mandy, who gave me an out of character high five as I hit the last stair.

"Mr. Gilford, we can't thank you enough for deciding not to sell the inn."

The other staff members echoed her comment, and it felt good to be around what I had discovered to be a real family of people. We relied on one another at the inn, and though it had taken me a long time to understand that, my mother had been right all along. These people were family, and it felt good to have them all smiling at me.

"Thanks, everyone! We'll be having an employee appreciation day sometime next month. I don't want to spoil it for you, but it's going to be a blast. If anyone has any suggestions since I know my mother used to do them with you guys, please let me know. You know where to find me."

With calls and echoes of "Thanks, Mr. G!" in the air, I walked away with a smile and a wave to sit beneath the tree that overlooked the valley below. I'd begun referring to it as Our Spot in my mind because it was where Becca and I had shared that Fourth of July picnic together. It felt like so long ago, and I missed her more than I liked to admit. Nearly every inch of the inn and the surrounding grounds seemed to be haunted by the memory of the woman I shouldn't have lost.

It had been my fault she left, but that didn't made it any less difficult to bear. In fact, it made it that much worse. I would often go to that spot to relax, and naturally, my mind would drift to all we'd been to each other. Though I missed her, I had to admit it was really over. I'd left her dozens of different messages for days after she stormed out, but she never called back.

But even if she didn't know it, what she said about selling the inn and putting all my staff out of their jobs sunk in. It wasn't the right thing to do, and when it came time to sign on the dotted line and leave the inn, Vermont, and all the memories of the past year behind, I couldn't do it.

I sat with my back pressed against the bark of our tree and stared out at the valley and all the trees that surrounded it with their red and gold colors. Vermont really showed off in autumn. I hadn't noticed last year, and as I took it in now, I couldn't help but wish that I could be enjoying the beauty with Becca.

CHAPTER TWENTY-FOUR

Becca

O NCE BACK IN the city, I didn't think about the little inn tucked away on its mountain or the man who had broken my heart who owned it. When fall began to come to New York City, I found my thoughts drifting back to that place, though. The leaves in Central Park began to change, but they didn't hold the same power over me as the ones that floated down over that little red bridge near the inn. Still, I pushed those thoughts down and focused on my work, getting more done daily than I had thought was humanly possible.

"You miss him, huh?" Amy asked me one day as I held the door open for her to leave for the night.

I locked the door behind us and shook my head. "Not really. I mean, there were some really good times, but I think I miss that inn more than anything. Now that he's sold it, I don't even really connect the two together in my mind anymore."

Amy gave me a look that told me she knew I was lying but being the great friend that she was, she didn't say anything more. That's how it went for the most part. I'd go to work, get everything done, go home, and fall asleep to the glow of the television as I wondered how much longer I would even get to live in my perfect little townhouse. Dustin's lawyer turned out to be as relentless as her reputation claimed, and she slowly had worn me down.

One crisp autumn day, I got home from work and wrapped myself in a warm blanket to thumb through the day's mail. That was when I saw it.

The postcard.

Similar to the campaign I'd designed, it featured a photograph of the beautiful fall leaves in all their colorful glory and the words, "We hope you and your family will join ours and enjoy autumn with us at The Gilford House Inn."

As I sat alone in my townhouse, I recalled how much I loved going up to Vermont in the fall. Before I knew it, I had packed my bags and I was making the familiar trek up there. As I drove, I realized I probably wouldn't be able to get a room on such short notice, but that didn't change my mind about going. I just wanted to see what the new owners had decided to do with the place.

When I got there, I saw things looked mostly

the same, though they'd given the outside of the building a fresh coat of white paint. It looked as welcoming as it ever did, standing proudly atop its mountain. I decided to take a stroll around the grounds before finding out if I could get a room, happy to just enjoy the beauty the area offered.

As I explored the grounds, I naturally thought of Zane. He was probably enjoying the California coast and all the fun and sun at the beach. I didn't feel any bitterness towards him at that moment, though. Only a sadness for the times that we'd had and lost. It didn't hurt anymore to admit that I missed him, and I even smiled as I looked out to where I knew we'd had our last little picnic together.

It had been such a marvelous time, but that's how it was with us. Things were great when they were good between us. I found myself back on that little red bridge, which also seemed to have been given a fresh coat of paint. That made me happy. The new owners cared about the little things.

As I walked to the other side of the bridge, I heard footsteps join me on it from behind and I instantly recognized the voice that said, "I remember having quite an argument on this bridge."

Shocked, I turned around to see Zane smiling at me.

"What are you doing here?" I asked, not even trying to mask my confusion.

Zane looked better than ever with a fresh haircut and shave and wearing a dark blue button down shirt that showed off his muscles. Crossing the bridge to stand on my side, he said, "I didn't sell the place after all."

"Why?"

He looked around and smiled, his eyes lingering on our spot under the tree I'd been thinking about just moments before. "It seemed like the right thing to do."

"The right thing, huh?" I said as he took another step closer to me. "What about doing the year and then going as you planned? I thought you didn't like it here."

He nodded, and with a shrug said, "I didn't until you became a part of this place. When the time came, I couldn't give it up, even if I'd lost you."

"I'm glad you didn't, Zane. What about the staff? Are they all still here?"

"Yep. Mandy's still at the front desk, and those two diva chefs are still making my life difficult in the kitchen."

"You look good here. Happy."

Our conversation felt awkward, like there was so much more to say and neither one of us knew how to say it.

"I guess I grew to love the place. My mother is probably looking down and laughing at the irony. I spent all my life wanting to get away from here, and now that I can go anywhere in the world, I'm staying right here."

I looked around and smiled. "I can't think of a better place to be than right here. I bet she's not laughing. I bet she's happy. You did this place right, Zane."

"Thanks."

We stood there staring at one another, and as much as I wanted to say more, I didn't. "Well, I think I'm going to go. Good luck with everything, Zane."

I turned to walk back to my car, but he touched my arm and said, "Don't go. You belong here. You belong with me."

Nothing sounded better, but after all we'd been through, was it even possible?

"I love it here, and if I'm being completely honest, I still love you. But I don't know. I just don't know, Zane."

He stepped toward me and slid his arm around my waist. Instantly, my body melded to his, and I loved the feel of his strong arm holding me.

"I'm guessing you didn't think you were going to see me, but since we both feel the same way as we did, can't we try again?"

I looked away, too much emotion welling up inside me to keep staring into those deep brown eyes of his. "I secretly wished I would see you, even though I was pretty sure you had left for California and never looked back."

Gently, he placed his fingers on my chin to turn my face back towards him. Placing a kiss on my forehead before pressing his own to mine, he said, "I missed you, Becca. Give me another chance to show you I am the man you hoped I was. Give me a chance to show you I love you."

CHAPTER TWENTY-FIVE

Zane

MY EYES SNAPPED open at the sound of the alarm blaring in my ear, and I felt like a kid on Christmas morning. Quickly, I slammed my hand down on it to turn it off and stretched my body. The sun shone through the curtains, and I rolled over to gently shake Becca's shoulder until her eyes fluttered open.

"Hey, today's the big day. You need to get up."

She smiled up at me and said, "You sure you want to do this? It's a big step you know."

I hopped out of bed and in minutes I was ready to greet the world. Heading towards the door, I replied, "It's the right thing to do. I'll meet you down there."

Bounding down the stairs, I hit the lobby and smiled at Mandy and her new assistant as I walked into the dining room.

"Today's the day right?" Mandy called over

cheerfully.

"Sure is!" I said, earning a smile from the two of them.

I sat down at the table where I'd first seen Becca and waited for her there. When I saw her coming toward me, it struck me once again how beautiful she was. It didn't matter if she was in her professional work clothes or jeans and a t-shirt. She never failed to stun me.

Standing, I took her hand in mine and kissed her softly. "You ready?"

She answered with a simple nod, and I planted one more kiss on her forehead as I breathed in the smell of her lavender shampoo and then walked out onto the front porch with her. Kristen, my attorney, waited for us looking supremely uncomfortable and out of place in one of the old rocking chairs that sat alongside a small table at the end of the porch.

"Good morning, Kristen. I appreciate you coming out to meet us here today. Would you like to come inside and have a coffee?"

Kristen smiled politely. "No, thank you. It's a very nice New England fall day, so if you're fine out here, so am I."

She wore her usual dark colored pantsuit and her hair sat on the top of her head in a tight bun. She looked like she would rather be anywhere else than in a chair that moved despite her wanting it to remain still.

"I'm sorry Zane had you come all the way out here," Becca offered as she shook Kristen's hand. "But it really is lovely to see you again. How is everything in town? I hear you're moving out to Boston to relocate permanently."

"I am. My father needs some help at home since his surgery. I'll be visiting a lot, though, trust me. Anyway, let's get down to business."

We sat down in the chairs around the small table and listened as she instructed us on what we needed to do. Pointing at the signature lines on the back page of the legal agreement she'd set out on the table, she said, "I just need you to sign here and here, and you will officially be joint owners of The Gilford House Inn."

We took turns signing the document and exchanged a long glance after we were finished. Co-owners of our little piece of heaven.

"Excellent. Congratulations! You're now joint owners. Enjoy!" Kristen said with a smile, shaking our hands.

"Are you sure we can't invite you in?" Becca asked, reading my mind.

Kristen waved off the offer. "I wish I could, but I have a ton of work to do. Good luck you two. It's a great place, so I know you'll be happy."

She hurried off after we thanked her for her help, and I turned to Becca. "So now we own this place. Are you sure you aren't like Kristen there, regretting leaving the big city and your advertising career for this sleepy inn here in the sticks?"

Becca shook her head before leaning in and kissing me. "I love this place, and I love you, Zane Gilford. So no, I don't regret a thing. What about you? Any regrets about not going back to the perpetually sunny days of California?"

I shook my head, more sure than ever that I'd make the right choice. "No way. I can't think of anywhere else in the world I'd want to be but right here."

She leaned in and gave me another kiss as my mind drifted off for a moment to thoughts of all the times, good and bad, that I'd had at the inn and how it had all come to this. My mother had always wanted me to love the inn as much as she had, and now I did.

Silently I said to myself, "Thanks, Mom. I hope I showed you that you didn't fail to do right with me. I hope I made you proud."

Becca said something, but I didn't hear her since I'd been wrapped up in thought. I looked down at her as she rested her head on my shoulder and said, "Sorry, babe. I didn't hear you. What did you say?"

"Where were you there? You looked like you were a million miles away just now," she said with that playful little smile of hers that I loved so much.

I shook my head and kissed her. "Nope. I'm right here. Right where I belong."

KEEP READING FOR MORE ON K.M.'S BOOKS

The Corrupted Love Trilogy:
If I Dream, If You Fight, and If We Fall

Ryder and Serena's unforgettable story of passion, crime, and the lengths you go to for love. Start it today with If I Dream and see why readers LOVE this story! Read the first chapter here!

IF I DREAM
CHAPTER ONE

Ryder

A S USUAL, THE crowd at The Pit screamed its
lust for the two of us to pound the fuck out
of each other. Impatient bastards. I couldn't hear
any one person's words clearly, but I'd done this
enough times to know what the people who'd
come to watch us wanted.

Blood. Pain. And one of us as close to death as
possible. It thrilled them in some sick way almost
as much as I suspected winning did when their
fighter crushed another person.

My opponent tonight stood nearly as tall as I
did at six foot three, but his body was smaller than
mine. He looked older, like something in the way
he carried himself said he'd seen more of life than
I had. His angular face looked hard, and on either
side of his perfectly straight nose were eyes staring
me down like he thought squinting and grimacing
would make me run for the nearest exit like some
fucking scared little boy. He was fighting the

wrong person if that's what he expected.

I'd never lost and for good reason. When you had nothing but the feel of your fists beating the hell out of someone and the sound of those rabid fucks cheering you on like you were some kind of hero for nearly killing another man, all you wanted was to win.

Fifteen times I'd won right here in this dank warehouse against guys bigger and stronger than me, and every time it seemed to surprise everyone. Even those who had bet on me.

If they only knew how unlikely it was anyone could match the rage inside me, they'd never bet against me again.

Some impatient bastard behind me barked, "Stop dancing around! Hit 'em!"

Mr. Grimace narrowed his eyes until he could barely see out of them and took a deep breath. Why did he bother with all this tough guy bullshit? That's not what these bloodthirsty fucks wanted.

Pain is what they wanted.

So that's what they'd get. His or mine. It didn't matter to them.

"Scared, motherfucker?" he grunted out in a deep voice I knew wasn't really how he talked. "I'm going to fuck you up."

I didn't bother answering.

He caught me in the face with a hard right

that scrambled my brains for a second, and then his fist skidded along my jaw and ran square into my right shoulder. The last guy I fought had done a number on that one, so that hurt like a bitch.

I knew how this went, though. The people around us wanted a show as much as they wanted a fight. I could have just beat the fuck out of him and won, but that's not what this was. I'd been told that enough times to understand even if I could pound the piss out of a guy, I had to at least make it look like a fight and not just some sad beat down.

So that's what I did. I took a few hits, sometimes more than a few, and let it look like there was some chance I wouldn't win. The other guy got to feel pretty big in the shorts and the crowd got to feel like this was really a match between two fighters.

It wasn't, though.

He paraded around like a peacock, preening to the crowd while I gritted my teeth and pushed my shoulder back into place. I took a deep breath and waited for the moment I'd show him who he was dealing with.

Flush with the love of the crowd, he turned back to face me. A few shots into me had made him think he had a chance.

I stepped forward as he lunged at me and leveled my fist against his jaw. His head ricocheted back, sending him reeling for a second or two, but I didn't let up. My right hand zeroed in on his face again, this time connecting with his cheekbone. I felt it crack against my knuckles bulging out of my fist and saw him stagger back away from me.

But he would get no mercy from me. That wasn't what I was here for.

"Get him!" the crowd screamed as the guy cowered, hanging his head to protect his busted face.

That wouldn't help him, though. Not with me. I knew what my role was. I knew why all these people had come here tonight, and it wasn't to see mercy. Mercy was for suckers. Fuck mercy.

They wanted blood and pain, and blood and pain is what they'd get.

I walked toward him as a feeling of complete calm came over me. All the noise of the crowd around us faded away until all I heard were the words I told myself every time I stood to fight.

It's you or him. Nothing more. Either you win or he does, but if you lose, you'll have nothing.

He looked up and I saw the pleading in his eyes. I'd seen it fifteen times before. No matter how big and tough they'd been in the beginning, each one ended up giving me that same sad look that said they wanted me to be someone other than who they'd heard I was.

Someone other than who I had to be.

Maybe they fought for some reason that had nothing to do with their very survival. Maybe they thought it would be fun, or it would make them feel tough. Maybe they thought they had something to prove to some girl. Whatever their reasons for agreeing to fight, they weren't why I fought.

For me, every win put me one step closer to being free. I didn't fight for shits and giggles or because I wanted to impress some skirt. I fought for the chance that one day I would never have to step foot in this fucking shithole place again. I fought because deep in the back of my mind there existed the tiniest dream that one day I'd be normal and have a normal life.

That one day I wouldn't have to be the man I'd been forced to become in this fight.

I knew his weak spots and attacked them. My fists pummeled his face, and no matter how hard he tried to shield himself from the blows, it was no use. Over and over, I hit him until that pretty face of his looked like mangled hamburger. Blood, flesh, and bone mixed to make a horror show. The nose that had been so straight just a few minutes before now pointed down toward his mouth like some deranged compass.

As I stood up to my full height, I heard the crowd cheering, as if I'd done something worthy of praise. A man lay in a crumpled heap at my feet, defeated and broken, and these fuckers were thrilled about it.

Looking around, I saw some clapping and others pumping their fists in the air as my win filled them with some kind of messed up happiness. Who was I kidding? What it filled was their wallets. That's why they were so happy.

Floyd raised my right arm in the air to the delight of the rabid fans and said in my ear, "That's my boy. You done good, son."

I forced a smile and nodded my head. I wasn't his boy and he wasn't my father. I was his fighter and he was the scumbag who went out to find people for me to fight. Whatever else he thought we were was all in his mind.

He lowered my arm and slapped me on the back. "Go relax. You deserve it. You put on a good show. Just look at the way these people love you!"

I tore my stare from his greasy comb-over and beady eyes and looked over his head to see the people who loved me. Between the booze, the drugs, and the fight, they looked like wild animals.

Who was worse? Them or me?

"RYDER, THERE'S SOMEONE here to talk to you," Floyd yelled from the other side of the door.

I didn't want to talk to anyone. All I wanted to do was sit on my crappy metal folding chair in this dingy room and hope my shoulder started feeling better. I'd downed a few shots of Floyd's whisky about ten minutes ago, but so far, it hadn't helped ease the pain.

"Not now," I yelled back.

He'd only open the door anyway. I knew that. It still felt good to let him and whoever the hell was standing there with him know that I didn't want to talk.

The door opened a second later and I saw Floyd and some guy who looked far too well-dressed to be anywhere near the warehouse on any night standing in my shitty little room. He had a vibe that screamed money with his suit, expensive shoes, and slicked back grey hair that made him look what my mother used to call stately.

"This is Mr. Robert Erickson," Floyd said as the man walked into the room like he owned the place. "I'll leave you two to talk."

I'd never seen Floyd leave a scene that fast. As he closed the door, I looked at the man who stood in front of me and saw he was studying me as much as I was him. Not that I was all too curious about what he wanted. People dressed like he was coming into my world never brought anything good with them.

Never.

The intruder looked around the cinder block room I called mine and then looked down at me. "Ryder, as our mutual friend Floyd said, my name is Robert Erickson. Do you know who I am?"

Shaking my head, I shrugged. "Nope. Should I?"

His dark eyebrows drew in like angry black slashes and his eyes narrowed to slits, much like the way the guy I just beat to a pulp had looked at the beginning of our fight. "I'm the man who runs this show. You are sitting in my warehouse and fighting in my stable. So yes, maybe you should know who I am."

As much as I knew he thought I should be impressed by this, I wasn't. Folding my arms across my chest, I said, "Oh yeah? Nice to meet the big boss then. I hope you bet on me tonight."

His eyes opened wider as the corners of his mouth inched up into what reminded me of how a crocodile looked right before he ate his prey. "You're pretty sure of yourself, aren't you?"

I looked up at the ceiling for a moment, unsure how I should answer that. Fuck yeah, I was sure of myself. I may not have been wearing a thousand dollar suit and fine leather shoes like him, but I had gifts of my own that had made me a winner sixteen times already.

Pursing my lips, I shrugged again. "I haven't lost yet. Come see me when I do and I'll tell you how cocky I'm feeling then."

His crocodile smile spread even wider across his face. Nodding, he said, "I'll remember that. For now, I'm here to tell you I've bought your contract from Floyd. So now you work for only me."

The words hit me like a fist to the face. I didn't have a contract with Floyd or anyone else. I fought to pay off money I owed him, and when that debt was paid off, I'd get to leave this shithole world of fighting. Now all that seemed like a pipe dream this fucker had dashed to pieces.

I stood from my rusted metal chair and stared at Robert Erickson. "What does that mean?"

Nearly the same height, he met my gaze with one so intense I thought about taking a step back. When he spoke, it sounded like his voice came from somewhere dark.

"It means I own you now. You fight for me and I expect you to win like you always have."

Left unsaid was the implicit threat that hung off every word. If you lose, you'll suffer. The only question was how.

My mind spun at the news that all I'd planned, all I'd worked for, was gone now. "So I guess my deal with Floyd to be released from fighting when I paid off what I owed him is gone too?"

"Yes."

"And if I don't agree to this new deal?" I asked, silently gauging my chances of not only getting past him but finding some way of surviving after I got away. He was big, and I had a sneaking suspicion even bigger guys stood outside waiting for him.

Robert Erickson looked like the type of man who got what he wanted, one way or another, whether the other person involved wanted it or not.

"You have no say in it, but let me assure you that you want to fight for me. For now, let's get you to your place so you can pack your things."

He turned to open the door as I explained this room was my place. "No need to go anywhere. You're already in it."

Erickson slowly looked back at me with confusion written all over his face. "You live here?"

I nodded. "Yeah. Short commute time to work and everything I need within arm's reach. What more could a guy ask for?"

Closing the door, he turned to face me. "How old are you?"

"Eighteen."

"And you live here, in my warehouse where Floyd holds fights for me?" he asked as he looked around my room again, this time with a look of disgust like the fact made him sick.

"Yep. Better than the street or jail. I might not get three hots, but I got a cot and a shower."

My answer didn't make the sickened expression leave his face, but he nodded anyway. "Well, gather your things. It's time to go."

I opened my mouth to ask where, but he walked out and left me standing there in that room I'd lived in for the past three months. As I stuffed the few clothes I owned, deodorant, and my toothbrush into a duffel bag, I thought wherever I was going had to be better than this place.

WE PULLED UP to a massive black gate between two even bigger rows of hedges and stopped momentarily as the driver got the go ahead to drive onto the property. I couldn't help but stare out the window as we drove up the long driveway past some kind of fountain that looked like something the Greek gods might swim in and a bunch of smaller hedges than the ones out front that looked like the gardener had cut them all into bird shapes. Robert Erickson was even richer than I'd first thought. Only insanely wealthy people lived in places like this.

The car stopped in front of a house so big I couldn't see all of it as I looked out the car window. Erickson tapped me on the arm as I stared out at the mansion and said, "Welcome home."

Home? This couldn't be my home. Instantly, the thought of what I'd have to do to live in a place like this raced through my mind. Fighting in The Pit wasn't going to be enough to live in a house like the one I saw in front of me.

I opened the car door and stepped out onto a stone driveway as I gaped at the house, which was even more impressive without the tinting of the car window getting in my way. Huge white columns towered above us to the second story of the gold colored home, and a glass front door so enormous I'd never seen one so big stood behind them.

"Follow me," was all Erickson said as he led the way to those doors. I couldn't imagine what waited inside after an outside this incredible.

I did as he ordered and caught up to him as he walked into an entryway so big the sound of our shoes hitting the white marble tile on the floor echoed off the matching marble tiled walls. He strode through like nothing around us was special toward the most spectacular curved wrought iron staircase I'd ever seen.

Not that I had seen many curved staircases with wrought iron in my life. I think I'd seen either a grand total of two times in a magazine some girl had in English class one time. I really didn't have much interest in reading architectural magazines, but she did and since I wanted to get in her pants, I sat next to her after school as she told me all about her dreams of having a huge house with a curved staircase and a wrought iron railing one day.

She would have loved Erickson's place. For me, it made me feel small, something very few people or things had achieved in a long time. Not small, actually. More like insignificant.

As my head swiveled left and right to look at the artwork on the walls, Robert said, "Come in here to my office. I want you to meet some people."

My hand clutched the handle of my duffel bag tightly in my palm. Meet some people? I didn't even look like they'd let me on the property to be the goddamned gardener who made hedges into animal shapes and now he wanted to introduce me to some people?

That feeling of insignificance morphed into one of pure discomfort. I didn't belong there, no matter how much he wanted to parade me through the place, and whoever he wanted me to meet would know that as sure as I did.

He led me into his office, a room even bigger than the entryway and as dark as that was light. This room had dark green walls the color of a pool table and a dark wood floor. Floor to ceiling bookcases held books with names I'd never heard of and sculptures I guessed cost more than my life was worth.

"Wait here. I'll be right back," he announced before leaving as I continued to look around in awe.

Seconds later, he came back with two females and ordered them into his office. Neither one looked like him, but something about the way they acted told me they weren't servants or people he'd just basically bought, like me.

They stopped dead at the sight of me standing there in my old gym pants and black t-shirt and the one I figured was older spun around to look at him in disgust.

"Who is this?"

"Girls, this is Ryder. He's going to be living here, so treat him like family."

Robert's proclamation infuriated her, and she shook her head angrily. "What, like a brother? You go out one night and get us a brother? Is that how it goes, Dad?"

He ignored her outburst and turned his two daughters to face me. "Ryder, the one who can't stop talking is Janelle. The other one is Serena."

"Hi," I mumbled, unsure if I should say anything.

They both stood staring at me like I was some foreign thing that needed to be removed and fast. The one named Janelle had short dark brown hair, and although I couldn't be sure since her eyes were flashing so much hatred, I thought they were brown too. Thin, she wore jeans and a tight blue shirt and heels that gave her at least three inches on her normal height.

The other one, Serena, had lighter brown hair that fell to below her shoulders in soft waves that reminded me of what mermaids looked like. Dressed in jean shorts and a white t-shirt that both showed off her tan and toned body, she stood barefoot next to her father and stared at me with big brown eyes that didn't have hatred but something else in them.

Disappointment?

As Janelle returned to complaining about my very existence, I heard Serena say in a pained voice, "You said you knew where she was. You promised you'd find her this time. Where is she?"

I imagined that's what that guy with the pleading eyes would have sounded like if he begged me not to beat the shit out of him. The way she said those words made my chest hurt, and I didn't even know who she was talking about.

But Robert was unmoved by her pleading. Waving off her questions, he said, "Maybe next time, honey. For now, I want you two to welcome Ryder to our home."

He put his arms around both of them, but Janelle slipped out of his hold and stormed off without another word. I didn't have to guess how she felt about me. Serena said nothing more about what was obviously so important to her and simply looked at me with that pleading in her eyes that hadn't worked on her father.

With a nudge from him, she finally said, "Welcome to our home. I hope you like it here."

And with that, she quietly left without another word to her father about whoever she wanted him to find.

Robert walked behind his desk and sat down in his chair as I watched her walk away, her sagging shoulders signaling how defeated she felt. Clearly, it didn't affect her father at all.

"They'll get used to you. Janelle is a little temperamental, but I guess that's to be expected from a girl, even one her age. She's a lot like me, though, so at least she has that going for her. Serena is the polar opposite. She's like her mother. Don't worry about her. She'll take to you like every stray she brings home."

Not that I didn't know I looked like some stray dog compared to them, but the way he said it brought the reality home for sure. In a hurry to get out of there and to wherever he kept the strays he brought home, I said, "Well, if you can just point me in the direction of where you want me to go, I'll get out of your hair."

He shook his head as that crocodile smile

spread across his face again. "Not yet. First, I want you to know what I expect of you. So sit down and relax."

Dropping my duffel bag, I sat down in a chair in front of his desk as he'd ordered and listened to hear just what this whole arrangement would involve.

He steepled his fingers in front of him and began. "You'll continue to fight as you did tonight. As I said before, I expect you to continue to win. When you do, you'll get paid, despite the fact that you won't need money as long as you live here."

"I won't need money?" I asked, confused what kind of world this guy lived in that didn't require cash.

Lifting his chin, he shook his head. "No, you won't. Your room and board, along with all the food you want and clothes you need, will be provided. I have a state of the art workout center you're to use to make sure you're in the best shape possible. So you see, you won't need money."

I didn't know if I should question this whole situation that sounded too good to be true, but I asked, "And if I don't win a fight?"

His face grew dark. "Let's cross that bridge when we come to it. For now, I have very few rules, other than you performing in fights like I've seen. No drugs and no romantic attachments. I don't care who you fuck, but don't get involved. I remember being your age, so I don't expect you to live like a monk, but no relationships."

I wasn't a fan of having so much of my life dictated, but assuming I got a room even as big as a broom closet on his estate, maybe it wouldn't be too much of a tradeoff. I wasn't exactly looking for a relationship anyway and I didn't do drugs. Hoping he wasn't about to announce that I had to double as a stable boy or something like that, I smiled.

"Okay. I can live with those."

"And you aren't to tell anyone here what you do. Is that clear?"

"Sure. But if I'm not here as a fighter, what am I supposed to say if someone asks?"

"They won't," he said with a confidence I guessed came from being the boss.

"Got it."

"Good. I'll have my housekeeper take you to your room. For now, you'll have the spare bedroom on this floor."

A short, dark haired woman he called Josephine appeared a few seconds later, so I stood from my chair and grabbed my duffel bag to go with her. I felt like there were a lot more questions I should ask Robert, but he didn't seem interested in talking anymore and picked up the phone to call someone, so I smiled again and moved to leave.

Just before I reached the door, he said, "Oh, Ryder, one more thing."

There it was. The one thing that would make this whole situation unbearable. I slowly turned around and waited for the other shoe to drop.

"Don't even think of doing anything with either of the girls. In that respect, I do care who you fuck."

I thought back to how much Janelle hated me already and easily put the idea of fucking her out of my mind. And Serena? I wasn't sure if she was even legal, and I didn't need that dogging me. An angry father was one thing, but prison was an entirely different story.

She was beautiful, though. There was something about her I could definitely like, if things were different. But no matter how beautiful she was, I wasn't touching that.

"No problem," I answered with confidence, hoping that was the worst thing about living at Erickson's house.

If it was, this would be the best thing to ever happen to me, even if it meant I had to keep fighting. Maybe freedom wasn't all it was cracked up to be anyway.

GET YOUR COPY OF
IF I DREAM TODAY!

ABOUT THE AUTHOR

K.M. Scott writes contemporary romance stories of sexy, intense, and unforgettable love. A New York Times and USA Today bestselling author, she's been in love with romance since reading her first romance novel in junior high (she was a very curious girl!). Under her Gabrielle Bisset name, she writes erotic paranormal and historical romance. She lives in Pennsylvania with a herd of animals and when she's not writing can be found reading or feeding her TV addiction.

Be sure to visit K.M.'s Facebook page at **facebook.com/kmscottauthor** for all the latest on her books, along with giveaways and other goodies! And to hear all the news on K.M. Scott books first, sign up for her newsletter today and be sure to visit her website at **www.kmscottbooks.com**.

BOOKS BY K.M. SCOTT:

Hard Work

If I Dream (Corrupted Love #1)
If You Fight (Corrupted Love #2)
If We Fall (Corrupted Love #3)

Crash Into Me (Heart of Stone #1)
Fall Into Me (Heart of Stone #2)
Give In To Me (Heart of Stone #3)
Heart of Stone Volume One Box Set
Ever After (Heart of Stone #4)
A Heart of Stone Christmas (Heart of Stone #5)
Return To Me (Heart of Stone #6)
Forever With Me (Heart of Stone #7)
Heart of Stone Volume Two Box Set

Temptation (Club X #1)
Surrender (Club X #2)
Possession (Club X #3)
Satisfaction (Club X #4)
Acceptance (Club X #5)
The Complete Club X Series Box Set

Crave (Addicted To You #1)
Adore (Addicted To You #2)
Shatter (Addicted To You #3)
Claim (Addicted To You #4)

K.M.'S BOOKS ARE IN AUDIOBOOK TOO!

BOOKS BY GABRIELLE BISSET:

Vampire Dreams Revamped (A Sons of Navarus Prequel)
Blood Avenged (Sons of Navarus #1)
Blood Betrayed (Sons of Navarus #2)
Longing (A Sons of Navarus Short Story)
Blood Spirit (Sons of Navarus #3)
The Deepest Cut (A Sons of Navarus Short Story)
Blood Prophecy (Sons of Navarus #4)
Blood Craving (Sons of Navarus #5)
Blood Eclipse (Sons of Navarus #6)
The Sons of Navarus Box Set #1
The Sons of Navarus Box Set #2

Stolen Destiny (Destined Ones Duology #1)
Destiny Redeemed (Destined Ones Duology #2)

Love's Master
Masquerade
The Victorian Erotic Romance Trilogy

www.ingramcontent.com/pod-product-compliance
Lightning Source LLC
Chambersburg PA
CBHW021209250626
47155CB00008B/2748